"It's not right to want your best friend's wife."

Shock held Sharon frozen at his blunt declaration. Hadn't she struggled with the same thing as desire awakened all she'd been trying to keep sleeping?

"You should send me away as soon as I finish painting. Damn it, I don't want to be an adopted stray!" The words exploded out of Liam.

"You were Chet's best friend. Do you think he'd let you walk away without a job? A place to go?"

"Of course not."

"You're doing an incredible amount for me that wouldn't be getting done. I owe you big-time."

Liam remained silent, simply looking at her.

"And let's get one other thing clear," she said, stepping closer to him. "I'm not Chet's wife anymore. I'm his widow. That's a whole different thing. I got used to it—now *you* get used to it."

Dear Reader,

I've known women who've made the ultimate sacrifice: the loss of a husband on the field of battle. I'm also intimately acquainted with the sacrifices military wives make in general, as I was one for ten years. The long separations, the times you wish you could turn to someone and he's not there. Waking in the morning, seeing a pillow, and for just an instant thinking he's there only to realize he's not.

I am constantly concerned about the kind of care our veterans receive. Especially those with traumatic brain injury, some of whom never receive a wound that physically reveals the severity of their concussion. Many are far worse off than the hero in this book, and so many people have little patience for their problems.

These two people have lost a lot but find healing with one another. It's a healing I wish I could bring to everyone.

Hugs,

Rachel

THE WIDOW OF
CONARD COUNTY

RACHEL LEE

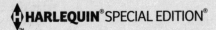

Recycling programs
for this product may
not exist in your area.

ISBN-13: 978-0-373-65752-0

THE WIDOW OF CONARD COUNTY

Printed in U.S.A.

Books by Rachel Lee

RACHEL LEE

was hooked on writing by the age of twelve and practiced her craft as she moved from place to place all over the United States. This *New York Times* bestselling author now resides in Florida and has the joy of writing full-time.

To all our wounded veterans,
many of whose wounds are not visible,
and to the families that love them and suffer with them.
May God bless you all.

Chapter One

Sharon Majors saw the man walking up the dusty drive to her house. No car, a knapsack on his shoulder, a slight dragging of his left leg.

Another drifter, common enough in Conard County, Wyoming during these hard times. Not a week passed that she didn't have someone show up at her door looking for work around her small ranch.

Not that she had much, usually. Since Chet had been killed in Afghanistan, she hadn't even had the heart to try to keep it up. She rented her grazing land to her neighbor, who pastured his sheep on it, while wind, sun and snow began to take their toll on outbuildings, fences and even the house. Lately she'd been trying to shake herself into taking some action about the deterioration.

But what did it matter? If she could sell the place

she would, just to escape all the memories. But people weren't buying small ranches these days.

Such dreams, she thought sadly. Chet had always wanted to have a small spread that he could work when he retired from the military. When he'd come home on leave four years ago, they'd settled on this one. Now those dreams were turning to dust and she just plain didn't care.

She watched the stranger come closer. She could afford to hire help to do some small things, but she almost never did because she knew nothing about these drifters. Instead, she'd sit them on the front porch, give them a sandwich or two and something to drink before sending them along.

The summer days were the hardest, when she didn't have her teaching to rely on to keep her busy. All her friends, free of the classroom, found excuses to get away, to visit family or take inexpensive vacations. She could have gone away, too, but a solitary vacation didn't interest her, and her family, such as it was, didn't really appeal to her. The years had turned her once-beautiful mother into an alcoholic, and her father into a man angry with life.

So she stayed here, knowing she was paralyzed and doing everything wrong, yet unable to take action. She told herself she couldn't abandon the ranch. But that was just an excuse. If she walked away from it, who would care?

She sighed and went to stand at the screen door, waiting for the man to reach her porch, to ask the inevitable question.

She was surprised, however, when he got close enough to make out details. Unlike most drifters who showed up here, he didn't look at all unhealthy despite that hitch in his gait. His dark hair was just a bit too long, not quite shaggy, and it looked clean. His face was careworn, but not pinched. And his clothes, ordinary denims and dusty boots, looked relatively new.

Had she been in a healthier frame of mind, she might have even thought him good-looking in a slightly rough sort of way. The flicker of attraction shocked her, and she quickly stomped down on it. She felt guilty enough for still breathing when Chet was gone. She wasn't going to make herself feel even guiltier with a momentary sexual attraction to a stranger. That part of her could stay dead and buried along with Chet.

She remained standing behind the door, the hook still latched, until he reached the porch steps.

He stood there for a minute, looking up at her, then he said words that turned her world upside down.

"You're prettier than the photo Chet had of you."

She gasped and grabbed the doorjamb as all the blood drained from her head. The world tunneled into darkness and spun.

"Crap," she heard him say as she began to sag. Dimly she was aware that he yanked on the door and swore again when the hook didn't yield. Then she heard another yank, heard wood splinter, felt strong arms grip her and steady her.

Those arms lifted her as he kept right on cussing himself. "Talk about ham-handed," he muttered. "No 'hello, I'm Liam,' no warning. No, just spit it out like a total idiot."

Her body suddenly remembered how to breathe, and she drew a deep, gasping breath just as he set her on the couch. Her whirling mind seized on one word: Liam. Chet's often-mentioned buddy. Liam.

Gradually the world came back into focus. Breathing helped, as did sitting down. Bit by bit, all the pieces came back together and the carousel in her mind slowed down.

Squatting in front of her was a large man, his face creased with concern. "You gonna be okay?"

"Yes. Yes." She closed her eyes a moment, gathering herself. "Just so unexpected."

"Yeah, I know. I was an idiot. I'm an idiot a lot these days." As she opened her eyes to look at him again, he tapped his head. "TBI."

"TBI?"

"Traumatic brain injury. I used to have more social skills."

"It's…okay." God, when had she lost the ability to talk? Shock, she told herself. The last thing she'd been prepared for was Chet's past to arrive on her doorstep today. She thought that chapter had been closed after the funeral, when the last condolences had been offered. Apparently not. "I'm fine," she managed after a moment or two. "I'm fine." Repetition made it sound like a mantra, and perhaps it was. She'd certainly whispered it to herself enough times.

"You still look pale," he said critically, but he retreated, standing across the small room, giving her space.

"You're Liam?"

"Yeah. Liam O'Connor. I guess Chet mentioned me."

"Many times. Please, sit."

He looked around and settled on the recliner that had been Chet's favorite. Her heart squeezed, and she told herself not to be ridiculous. Nobody had sat in that chair since the last time Chet was home, two years ago now, but it was ridiculous to treat a piece of furniture like some kind of memorial.

She hesitated, not sure what to say. What had brought him here after all this time? And a traumatic brain injury? God, one of the few things she had managed to be grateful for was that Chet hadn't faced that. Now here was his best buddy, sitting across from her, a victim of that very thing. She didn't know what to say, what to ask.

At this moment, just dealing with a ghost out of the past seemed to be testing her ability to cope.

"I, um, broke your door," he said. "Well, not the door, but I splintered the jamb." He looked down at his big hands, clenching and unclenching them. "Too much weight training, I guess. I'll fix it before I leave."

She started to tell him to forget it, but for some reason she felt that could be the wrong thing to say. "Uh, why too much weight lifting?"

He raised his head, and for the first time, she saw that his eyes were an unusual light green. "It was a way to work things out."

"Oh." She didn't know how to approach that, either. And he thought *he* was ham-handed.

"Look, I'm sorry. I should have called or something. But honestly, I didn't know how. Struck me as wrong to dump this over the phone. So instead, I show up and nearly give you a heart attack. Did I say I'm not so good socially anymore?"

Her heart squeezed again, but this time for him. She couldn't imagine what it must be like to have suffered a brain injury; couldn't imagine how that must have changed him and his entire life. "There was no good way," she said finally. "But why did you come?"

"I promised Chet." It sounded like the simplest answer in the world, but it wasn't. To Sharon, those words sounded heavy with significance. "I would've come sooner, but things kinda happened. I meant to be here on my first leave after he was killed, but I wound up in pieces, instead. Then it took me a while to get to the point where I could…I could…" He trailed off. Then, "I was in the hospital for a long time. Didn't much know whether I was coming or going."

"I'm sorry."

He shrugged. "Took me a while. To get well enough. To get my memory back, at least most of it. Then I found the letter."

"Letter?" Her heart almost stopped, then resumed beating nervously.

"Yeah, um… Are you sure I'm not going too fast for you? Maybe there's a better way to beat around this bush?"

"Better?"

He shrugged again. "Mrs. Majors, I don't know half the time anymore if I'm leaving stuff out, talking too fast, whatever. I'm doing better, but…" He shook his head. "So if I come on too strong, or skip things, just stop me, okay?"

"Okay." She waited. He didn't say anything, but seemed to turn inward. She wondered if she should just let him be or ask him to continue.

Then those light green eyes fixed on her again. "Sorry, I wander a bit, too, sometimes. Anyway, nothing like coming straight to the point, I guess. I don't seem to know any other way these days. Chet and I were buddies. But you know that. Like brothers. I always meant to come here with him to meet you, but we never got leave at the same time. He always talked about you, about this place after you got it. I remember thinking he was a little crazy."

"Crazy?" She didn't like that word.

He shrugged. "Not in a bad way. Just…different. I never met anyone else who talked about using a ranch to rescue animals."

"He really wanted to do that. All kinds of animals, not just pets."

"I remember. Sometimes when things were quiet, we'd lie there in our tent, or under the stars, or in a cave…hell, we slept just about everywhere. But he'd talk about all kinds of animals that didn't have good homes. He wanted to save them."

She nodded. "Yes, he did."

"Every time he talked about it, he was saving more of them. Last I heard, he was going to have a wolf pen and a whole herd of mustangs, too."

Sharon's mouth curved into an unexpected, unfamiliar smile. "I can just hear him."

"I never figured out how he'd keep wolves, though."

"We had forty acres he wanted to fence off just for a small pack."

"Well, if there was one thing I knew about Chet, he'd do it if he wanted to. He was like that."

"Yes, he was."

"Said he was going to use the place to teach folks."

"He wanted to give tours, mostly to school children."

Liam nodded. "Good idea. Anyway, I remember how those ideas used to get bigger every time we talked about them. I got the feeling he'd need more than one ranch."

That surprised a real laugh out of Sharon. "You're probably right. He always dreamed big."

"It was a way to pass some long nights." He paused. "I think I better get to it. I didn't mean to impose on you."

Get to what, she wondered uneasily. But he looked around, then said, "Guess I left my pack outside. Be right back."

She watched him cross to the front door and for the first time took in the splintered doorjamb. He'd pulled the hook right out. That was amazing, but it didn't frighten her. He'd done it to help her when she was fainting.

And that hitch in his step wasn't quite a limp, she noticed now. It was more like his leg didn't quite remember how to work.

He came back quickly, carrying his backpack, then resumed his seat with the pack on the floor in front of him. He opened a small pocket and reached in a couple of fingers.

"We gave each other letters to take home if something happened," he explained. Then he pulled out a small envelope and handed it to her.

She took it with her heart in her throat and turned it around until she could see her name written on it in Chet's familiar handwriting. And then she saw the brown spot on one corner.

She sucked in a sharp breath. "Blood?" The thought curdled inside of her.

"Not his," Liam said swiftly. "Mine."

She lifted her eyes, eyes that had begun to burn. "And that makes it better how?"

He didn't answer.

"Did you read it?" she asked, reluctant and eager all at once to open it.

"Hell, no. It was his private stuff for you. In case anything happened. Well, it happened, damn it."

"It sure did." She squeezed her eyes shut to stop the burning, then looked at him. "You could have just mailed it."

"I promised to deliver it personally." He rose suddenly. "Why don't I just wait outside while you read, and then I'll fix that door before I go."

Before she could summon a response, he vanished onto the front porch.

Her fingers trembled, and her heart seemed to be lodged firmly in her throat. Sixteen months, she reminded herself. Surely she could handle this after sixteen months. She'd handled the worst already.

And how many times had she wished she could hear Chet's voice one more time, get one more letter, one more something from the man she had loved as much as life? She doubted there was a single thing in that envelope that she didn't already know, things he just wanted to remind her of if he didn't come home. Things he had probably told her many times.

Carefully, slowly, she lifted the flap. With time, the glue had dried, and it almost popped open at her touch. Then she drew out a single, small sheet of paper, and felt her eyes flood as she saw his penciled handwriting.

Sharon, my dear, if you're reading this, well, it's obvious. I want you to know that I don't forget you for an instant out here, not one. No matter what's going on, you're on my mind. You're my home fire, the reason I keep going. All I ever really wanted was you, and all I want out here is to get back to you.

Just remember all the joy and happiness you've given me, all the happiness we shared. And when you remember that and remember me, remember also what I told you more than once.

Move on, Sharon. Make a life for yourself, find that happiness again. Because if you don't, my heaven will become hell.

Love forever,

Chet

Trembling, Sharon clutched the crinkly paper, then doubled over sideways on the couch and gave in to grief in a way she hadn't in a very long time. Deep, wrenching sobs escaped her, and the tears scalded her cheeks and soaked the couch. She felt as if the pain were tearing her in two.

Outside on the porch, Liam hesitated. Well, how had he expected her to react? If he hadn't been wounded, that letter would have been in her hands a year ago. Instead, it had arrived late and reopened *her* wounds.

The thing was, since he'd looked through his belongings before leaving rehab, that letter and the promise he'd made had been burning a hole in his mind, heart and soul.

"Maybe not so smart, buddy," he muttered to himself. Talking to himself had become a bit of a habit since it kept his thoughts on track. His condition was a whole lot better than six months ago, but he could still sometimes lose track of where he was in space and time. So he talked himself through things, and ignored the odd and uneasy looks many people gave him.

More than once over the past few weeks he had wondered if he should have ditched Chet's letter. But he'd made a promise to a buddy, and you didn't break those promises, even if you wondered if you would be walking in on a woman who had built a new life and didn't want to look back.

When he'd learned she still lived on the ranch, though, it had seemed to him that maybe she hadn't quite moved on yet. Maybe the letter would help.

Regardless, he had to keep the promise.

Then, horrifying him, he'd barely set eyes on her before he felt the stirrings of desire. For Sharon Majors. For his buddy's *wife*. God, she was a desirable woman, a small compact bundle topped by shaggy brown hair and a pair of eyes as blue as a gas flame. Parts of him he'd almost forgotten existed had sprung to life at his first sight of her. That sure as hell made him feel like a double heap of manure. He closed his eyes a second, filled with self-disgust. And guilt. Chet hadn't sent him here for *that*.

But now he was listening to her sobs and wondering why he and Chet had ever thought writing such letters would be a good thing. "Words from beyond the grave," Chet had called them. Yeah, and they came as such a shock. Maybe it wouldn't have been so bad if he'd been able to get here a few months after Chet died. But now it seemed awfully cruel.

His own letter had vanished with Chet, and that was just as well. Considering his sister, his only living relative, had given up on him after a few months when it had looked as if he was going to need to be spoon-fed for the rest of his days, he wouldn't have wanted that letter landing in her lap. Not now. Not ever.

The sound of the sobbing renewed and yanked him back to the here and now, thousands of miles away from Afghanistan, a year away from his sister's desertion. Not that he'd been much aware of it at the time. Later, after months of therapy that had helped him recover mobility, and much of his memory and speech, the VA helped him understand: his sister back home in Texas wasn't interested in looking after him.

And when it started to appear that he'd be able to take care of himself, he'd managed to let go of the hurt and make up his mind that he'd never count on anyone again.

He listened to those sobs and wished he knew what to do. Thing was, he was no longer sure what to do about most stuff. He'd gathered that his reactions were sometimes off, that he didn't always make himself understood and that socially he seemed to say a lot of the wrong things.

Somewhere inside he could remember a time when he didn't have those problems, but he couldn't remember them clearly enough. It was as if when he'd lost some of his function, his ability to remember *how* he had once functioned had almost completely evaporated with it. He just knew that he had.

He unleashed a heavy sigh of irritation and looked at the door. Instantly he remembered that he'd broken it and had promised to fix it. He stood there staring at it, trying to figure out what he needed to do and in what sequence and realized he absolutely couldn't.

A burst of savage frustration exploded in him. He'd brought a woman who was trying to mend to tears of anguish, and he'd busted a door and couldn't figure out how to fix it.

Nor did it help one damn bit to remember what the doctors had said when they'd cut him loose. How he'd come further and improved more than they'd ever hoped. That he would probably still improve.

It didn't help when he didn't know what to do about a woman's tears or how to fix a splintered piece of wood.

A cuss word escaped him too loudly. He knew he wasn't supposed to do that, but right now he damn well didn't care.

He ought to go back inside, grab his pack and leave this woman alone.

But he couldn't go back in there, not while she was still crying. Instead, he stomped away from the house along the rutted drive and tried to cool down.

Frustration was part of it. He knew that. He had to work it off now before it busted out of the cage and hurt someone or something.

At least he'd learned that much.

Sharon cried until she couldn't cry any more. When she finally sat up and wiped her face, her throat was raw and her diaphragm ached. God, she hadn't cried like that in nearly a year.

Liam was gone. At first she felt awful that she'd driven the man away when he'd just been keeping a promise, but then she saw his backpack was still on the floor in front of the recliner. So he hadn't left yet.

She should at least offer him coffee, a bite to eat. Be courteous enough to thank him for making this trek to the back of beyond to deliver a letter. It couldn't have been easy for him, either.

Besides, he'd been Chet's best buddy. Every single letter she'd gotten from her husband had mentioned something he and Liam had done together. Man, Liam must be feeling the loss as much as she, and she hadn't even acknowledged that.

She hurried to the bathroom to wash her face with cold water, but not even cold water could ease the puffiness around her eyes. Not that it mattered. Grief was an honest emotion, not something she needed to hide.

She saw the doorjamb again, splintered where the hook had pulled out of the wood. She regarded it for a moment, feeling it was somehow symbolic, but her brain was too cloudy from her crying jag to make sense of it.

Movement caught her attention and she saw Liam coming back up the dusty drive, just as he'd done before. Except this time she felt relief, relief that she hadn't driven him away. That would have been a mean thing to do.

He reached the porch steps and looked up at her, just as he had earlier. "You okay?"

"I'm fine. I'm sorry I drove you away."

"Wasn't you. I said I'd fix that door, but damned if I can figure out how."

She almost told him not to worry about it, but she caught a hint of frustration in his voice. TBI. Of course.

"How about we do it together?" she suggested. "I could use something to do with my hands. But first let's have a little to eat. I don't know about you, but I'm starving."

He hesitated only briefly before he mounted the steps and joined her inside. She noted for the first time that he was taller than Chet, and bigger in every other respect. Probably all that weight lifting he'd mentioned.

She led him to the kitchen, a sunny room with white cabinets, yellow walls and curtains and a laminate floor that stood up to spills. The first room she and Chet had finished after they'd bought the place. The rest of it she had worked on while he was gone.

She motioned him to the wood dinette with its ceramic-tile top, long a favorite of hers. "Anything you don't care for?"

He gave her half a smile. "Where I've been, you learn to be grateful for anything edible."

"I think I can do better than that. Are you a coffee drinker?"

"Can't live without it."

She started a fresh pot of coffee, then set about making sandwiches. Ordinarily she made small ones for herself, but this time she made two thick ham-and-cheese ones for Liam, the kind that Chet had always liked. For him, it hadn't been a sandwich unless it was loaded.

It felt good to be doing something for someone. For years now, her friends had made a practice of gathering here for a card game once a month, and except for a brief break when Chet had been killed, the tradition had continued. She always liked buzzing around making food for folks.

Her mood improved with the activity, and she was able to give Liam a bit of a smile when she served him his meal. She sat across from him, with her own little sandwich and coffee, and wondered where safe conversational ground lay.

"So were you on your way to somewhere?" she asked.

"No."

Half a sandwich in her hand, she paused. "You just came all the way here to deliver the letter?"

"Yeah. This sandwich is great. The best I've had in forever. Good coffee, too. Thanks."

"You're welcome." She watched him eat like a starved man while she chewed and swallowed a small bite herself, beginning to feel troubled. "Did you just get out?"

"Of rehab? Nearly a month ago."

"Family?"

He shook his head.

"Liam, what are you going to do?"

"I'll figure out something."

No plans, no family, fresh out of rehab with a traumatic brain injury. She didn't like the sound of that at all. She was no expert on the subject, but just drifting didn't sound good to her. As a teacher, she had occasionally dealt with people who suffered from cognitive deficits, and some of his statements made her certain that he suffered from some important ones.

"Well," she said slowly, knowing exactly what Chet would want her to do, and what she needed to do for a man who was willing to make a trip like this to keep a promise, "I could use some help around here. If you're not in a hurry."

He stopped eating. "I'm in no hurry," he admitted. "But I don't know how much help I'd be, Mrs. Majors."

"Sharon, please."

"Sharon. Honest to God, I don't know how much I can help. I need lists to keep me on track now. I have to talk to myself a lot to keep my train of thought going.

How can it possibly help you if you have to ride herd on me to get simple things done?"

She bit her lip, thinking, trying to avoid words that might give hurt when she intended none. "Well...looks like you have a strong back."

Again that half smile. "Yeah. Strong back, strong everything except for a weak brain."

"I don't think your brain is all that weak."

"You don't know."

"True. But I'll tell you what. Riding herd on you would be helpful for me."

He frowned. "How?"

"I need to keep busy, Liam. I've been letting this place go. My neighbors occasionally stop by and keep one thing or another from going to total ruin, but I hate depending on them, and I hate that I'm not doing it myself. You'd give me a reason to do the things I need to do."

His frown deepened, and she feared she'd said exactly the wrong thing. But it turned out he was parsing it through in his head.

"So you want to offer charity for charity?"

"I wasn't thinking of it that way, but I suppose you could."

"I don't want charity."

"Actually, neither do I."

"I don't want to be taken in like some stray dog."

"Hadn't even crossed my mind. Like I said, I've been letting this place go. You'd be doing me a favor to help me."

"Maybe. If I don't muck it up."

"You know what? I don't care if it gets mucked up. Messes can be fixed. I made enough of them to know.

The thing is, Liam, I need help. I need somebody to help me so I'll get back on track again."

"It's been rough for you."

It wasn't a question, but she nodded, anyway. "I haven't had the heart to keep the place up. I was thinking today that I really need to change that. You couldn't have arrived at a better time. But there's something else."

He lifted a brow. "What?"

"I don't want to hire a stranger to help me. I wouldn't be comfortable."

"I'm a stranger."

"Not really. Chet mentioned you in every letter he wrote."

He surprised her with a small smile. "Those paint chips you were always sending?"

She nodded again. "I wanted his color approval. He'd send back the ones he liked."

"Well, I'll bet he never told you what he did with the ones he didn't like."

"No. What?"

"We'd shoot them up."

She clapped her hand to her mouth, and then helplessly giggled. "Really?"

"Really. They were small enough to make it a challenge." He smiled again, and his gaze grew distant. "He sure did like getting those paint chips and fabric samples. We made some jokes, sure, but the truth was he liked them all. He liked being consulted."

"I'm glad." Chet had told her he liked being kept in the loop, but occasionally she had wondered if he was just being nice. She never did any decorating without consulting him, and an awful lot of paint chips, fabric samples and magazine photos had made their way out to him. As much as possible, she'd taken care to ensure he wasn't left out of any decision.

Her chest tightened again, but not with the tearing grief she had felt such a short time ago. No, this was the familiar ache she had learned to live with, still painful but endurable. A deep breath eased it a bit and she returned from memory to the present, the very empty present.

"Okay." Liam's quietly spoken word took her by surprise and she looked up at him quizzically.

"Okay," he said again. "I'll try to help you out. But you have to promise me something."

"What's that?"

"If it gets too hard on you, or if you have to corral me too much, you'll let me know and I'll move on. At this point, I still don't know all the things I can't do anymore. No idea whatsoever. I learn them as I go."

"We'll probably be learning a lot together. There's a whole bunch of stuff I haven't even attempted because I don't know how."

He cocked a brow. "I think I asked for a promise?"

She felt that ache again, and this time it wasn't for Chet or herself. "Okay," she said solemnly, "I promise."

A promise she had no intention of keeping if there was any way to avoid it.

She just knew she couldn't let this man drift on alone to God knew what. No way. She owed Chet more than that.

"Okay," he said again, and resumed eating.

It was settled.

Chapter Two

This far north, evenings were long. Sharon didn't feel like hunting up some half round to repair the door latch, although Liam seemed to want to get it done right away. Instead, she asked him to settle himself in the guest room, clean up in the hall bath if he liked and rejoin her for more coffee.

He studied her a moment before taking her directions. "Questions?" he asked.

"Questions?"

"About Chet?"

She paused, choosing her words carefully. "I think it would do us both some good to get a little more acquainted."

He frowned faintly, as if the prospect bothered him a little, but after a moment, he left to do as she'd asked. She listened to his footsteps climbing the stairs then walking around upstairs as he oriented himself. It gave her some time to think this through. She had to figure out his limits, had to understand how the injury had affected his temperament so she could deal with him in the best way possible for him.

She wondered how much he would even be able to tell her. Right now his life was probably a constant journey of discovery, finding his limitations and rediscovering his abilities. She needed to bone up on this whole subject, but not when he was looking over her shoulder. Later, she'd pull up what she could on her computer.

By the time he came back down, nearly an hour had passed. He'd showered and now was dressed in old uniform pieces: cammie pants, a black T-shirt and desert boots. A lot of soldiers didn't own much more than they could tuck in a duffel or footlocker, depending on their assignments. Too much hassle when your life left you wearing battle dress ninety-five percent of the time. Chet had left all his civvies here, but Liam obviously didn't have that choice. No family. Imagine that. Her heart ached for him. He needed *someone*.

They settled in the living room with fresh coffee, and he sat waiting, as if he expected an inquisition. Maybe that was what she was doing, and she shifted uncomfortably.

"You've told me," she said finally, "that you have trouble remembering things, figuring out how to do things. Is there anything else I need to know about?"

His brow knit. "How so?"

"I want us to work well together, so I need as good a picture as you can give me of your current condition."

"Oh." He sighed. "I think I told you I don't stay on task so well anymore."

"You stayed on task long enough to get here."

"That was simple. One step. All I had to do was figure out which way to go and then keep going. I can still read a map, and the map was my list."

"Anything else?"

"I have a temper. It's explosive now. I get frustrated easily. I work on controlling it, but don't be surprised if you hear me cussing a blue streak. I know I'm not supposed to do that, but sometimes I do it, anyway."

"I can handle that. Chet cussed a lot, too."

"I guess we all did."

"You seem to be pretty concerned about that doorjamb."

"I busted it." He paused. "Okay, I have trouble staying on task but sometimes I get pretty fixated on things. Like the door. A little of this, a little of that." He shrugged one shoulder. "I don't know it all yet. I'm still finding out."

"I guess we'll find out together, then." Her heart twinged as he sighed.

"Yeah," he agreed, "I suppose we will." His light green eyes grew distant. She let him be, waiting for whatever might occur to him next. As with some of her students, the only way to learn was often just to wait, listen and watch. She figured she had the easy part of this, by far. She couldn't imagine the pain if she had been sitting here talking to Chet in this condition. As it was, it was troubling enough.

"I saw sheep on the way in," he said. "I didn't know you had sheep."

"They belong to my neighbor. I lease grazing to him."

"Good idea. Chet wanted goats. Why goats?"

"He thought they were more fun. I don't personally know, since I never had any."

"That was going to be hard on you." His eyes fixed on her, telling her he was fully back from his wandering.

"Why?"

"You don't know anything about goats. How could you take care of them?"

A soft laugh, only half sad, escaped her. "Honestly, I think that was one of the many things he and I were going to worry about later."

"Yeah, after the castle was built in the air." A grin stretched his face.

She was surprised that he'd made that leap after the way he'd been criticizing his own capacities. "You only need the drawbridge after the castle is done."

He nodded. "That was Chet, all right. The most practical guy on Earth when it counted. But you know, I liked his dreams. Big dreams. Good ones."

"So did I." The shadow of sorrow passed over her once more, but she shook it away.

"Peaceful dreams," he added, looking down. "He was learning, too."

"Learning?"

"Yeah. He used to talk to the local farmers and goatherds when he could. Ask them to teach him. They really liked that."

Again, her heart squeezed. "He never told me that."

"Probably didn't want you getting frightened or something. I don't know. We were supposed to be winning hearts and minds. That's what they called it. But nobody did it like Chet. Or me," he added almost as an afterthought. "I don't know how many times he dragged me into helping some guy dig an irrigation ditch, or chase down some goats. All kinds of stuff. It was fun. And he kept saying he was learning."

All of a sudden he jumped up. "Sorry, I'm making you sad again. I need to learn not to ramble." Then he walked over to examine the door. "I need a long piece of wood like this, right?"

"Yes."

"What do you have out in that barn?"

She doubted she had any half round or even quarter round out there, but she could see no reason to stop him if he needed to look. "I don't know. I just go looking for stuff when I need it."

"I'll go look." He stared at the splintered wood again as if memorizing it, then walked out toward the barn. There was plenty of light left, and he'd surely find the switches just inside the barn door if he wanted more.

She watched him go, then wiped away a few of the tears she'd been holding in. Okay, he was determined to fix that door for her. Heading to the back of the house and her tiny office, she decided to look for drawings online. Something she could print out that he might be able to follow. Or at least that she could guide him through.

Liam verged on exploding again, and getting out of the house seemed like a damn good idea. Thinking about Chet made him angrier than a wet hornet, mainly because he always felt it would have been better if he'd taken that round himself. Chet had a real life. He should have lived to enjoy it.

Liam didn't have any life out of the army, really. None. The army was everything. He used to listen to Chet's stories like a kid staring at a toy he couldn't have.

He could remember that much, at least. It wasn't that he wanted Chet's life or Chet's wife, or anything, but he often got to wishing for a life, period. Something outside the big, green machine where he'd lived sixteen years since he turned eighteen.

Chet always made it seem like Liam was going to be part of that ranch he was dreaming up, but Liam figured he'd be no good at that, a city kid from Dallas. Still, it was fun listening and egging Chet on. Now look at him. Here he was, next to useless to anybody, and he figured the least he could do was try to help Chet's wife in some way.

As if he could. Damn, he felt like he *ought* to know how to fix that door. That was the most frustrating thing of all, looking at something he felt he ought to know and finding himself faced with some kind of jumble he couldn't seem to sort out. Like being dropped in a foreign land without a bit of knowledge of the language or customs.

And *that* was a feeling he knew for real. But never had it clouded damn near everything.

He was used to being clear on a lot. On his orders, on how to follow them, on what to do in most situations. He was used to being able to figure out things when he didn't know. Put pieces together.

Now everything was scattered like a million-piece puzzle, and he didn't know exactly where to start.

Well, that wasn't entirely true. He was putting more and more things together, however slowly. And understanding that he needed to walk out before the eruption hit was a big step.

The barn was shadowy and nearly dark inside despite windows. He felt for switches and flipped them on.

Then he spied some bales of hay near the door. Walking over, he punched them like a punching bag, working out the rage that plagued him too often.

As soon as the anger drained, fatigue hit him and he sat on one of the bales, studying his scuffed knuckles, trying yet again to come to terms with the man he had become. It wasn't easy. He could still remember that he hadn't been this angry in the past, at least not without good reason. Now it just rose in him like a tsunami, nearly coming out of nowhere.

In fact, he sometimes wondered if it was the only real, strong feeling he had left.

He flexed his hands, feeling their soreness, and sought for something firm and safe on which to fix himself. In rehab they'd taught him the technique, although he knew they had meant for him to use it before the rage took over. Unfortunately, sometimes he didn't get a whole lot of choice. It was a good technique, though, and helped him out often when the world seemed too jumbled.

Door frame. He'd busted her door frame. Find a piece of wood like the one he'd broken. He could do that, if there was a piece in here. Rising, he busied himself looking through piles of accumulated stuff, some of which he couldn't even remember the names for, if he'd ever known. This barn seemed to have been used for storage for a long time.

Figuring that much out made him feel good. Okay, it was a huge storage locker and like the puzzle in his brain, it was all jumbled up. He tried to make some order out of what he was seeing, but it took a long time.

He kept at it, though, and gradually the mess started to take shape. Hand tools hung above a long bench.

Wood along one side. Power tools nearby. Packages of shingles. Odds and ends it would take him more time to figure out. Larger pieces of machinery he couldn't identify yet.

Focus on the wood. There was quite a bit of it, and it seemed to be in pretty good shape. He wondered what Chet had been planning to do with it. Fence posts? He decided they must be, because he couldn't imagine any other use. He was relieved to recognize two-by-fours, two-by-twos and other pieces of lumber.

It wasn't all gone. No, it definitely wasn't all gone. The problem was imagining a plan for this stuff. Figuring out how to use it. Like looking at the door, knowing he could fix it, but being unable to remember how.

By the time he was done, he felt like his brain was smoking from overwork, but he was feeling pretty damn good, too. He'd sorted things out. He knew most of what he was looking at.

And at the very back, he found a piece of wood that looked like the piece he'd shattered in the doorjamb. Standing it upright, he measured it against himself and decided it was long enough.

He just hoped it wasn't intended for something else.

Then it hit him: Chet was gone. Whatever he had intended to do with this wood was gone with him.

Holding that slender piece of wood, he sat slowly on the bales again and closed his eyes. *Damn, Chet, I wish you were here. She needs you, not me.*

But he was all Sharon was going to get. A very poor substitute.

All of a sudden, he realized he was muttering under his breath. "Fix the door." Of course. He'd come out here for a reason. The reminder brought him to his feet and started him on the path to the house with wood in hand.

Fix the door. Such a simple thing, but such a big deal.

Sharon was relieved when she saw Liam coming back from the barn with a strip of wood in his hand. She had begun to wonder if she should go look for him, and hesitated only because she didn't want to make him feel any worse than he already did.

As short a time as she had known him, she'd gathered enough to know he'd suffered more than a TBI. His sense of self-worth had taken a major hit as well, and she could only imagine how this had to be affecting him emotionally and psychologically, apart from the physical injury. And, she reminded herself, he was grieving, too: for a best friend, and for himself.

He would never again be the man he had once been. That much she knew for sure. No one who suffered a TBI remained totally unchanged, and the worse the damage, the bigger the change.

Sadly, she realized she would never know the man Chet had called his best buddy. No, she would only get to know this new version of him. But maybe that was best for Liam. She would be making no comparisons, although she suspected he always would be making his own.

What a hell to live in!

When she heard the front door open and slam shut, she left her office, carrying the papers she had printed out. He stood inside the door with the strip of quarter round, holding it up beside the one he had splintered when he ripped the hook out. "It'll work," he said, as if to himself.

"Yes, it will," she agreed. "Was it hard to find?"

He turned to her. "Depends on what you mean by hard. I wandered around some, getting an idea of the place. There's a lot in there."

"Yeah. We were like squirrels storing up nuts, getting ready for..." She trailed off. Those plans were never going to come to fruition now. "We were planning ahead," she finished lamely.

"Good idea. That's something I need to learn again."

"We'll work on it," she said firmly, then realized what a commitment she was making. He didn't seem to notice, though, which relieved her. Neither of them knew how this was going to work or for how long.

She approached him with the papers. "Do these diagrams make sense to you?"

He took the papers, his brow furrowing. "It's all in pieces."

She wondered just what he meant by that. It was an "exploded" diagram showing the parts and how they were meant to fit together. Unnecessarily complex because the directions would have built a whole door frame. "Well, we'll work on it. I don't exactly get it, either." Then, after a hesitation, she decided to ask. "Liam?"

"Yeah?"

"Can you still read?"

The saddest thing for her was that he appeared embarrassed. "Not much," he admitted. "Mostly simple stuff."

"So you lost that, too. God." She didn't bother hiding her distress. "What's left, Liam? I'm amazed at how well you're dealing with this."

He seemed to pull back a little, then his stiffness

eased. "I'm still walking and talking. Too much talking sometimes. But I don't know, Sharon. There's a lot I don't know yet, and I don't know how much I'll get back. Are you sure you want me to hang around? I'll probably be more trouble than help."

The answer rose in her instantaneously, with no doubts. "I wouldn't want you hanging anywhere else."

"But I don't remember how to do a lot of things."

"And I don't have the muscles to do a lot of things." She reached out and playfully poked his arm. "Looks like you have plenty of power and a strong back. I'll use you mercilessly."

He surprised her by laughing. A genuine, easy laugh. "Use away. At least something still works right."

She fed them an easy meal, insisting the door could wait for morning. "It's been a stressful day for us both," she reminded him.

It certainly had been. The shock of meeting Liam, the bigger shock of the letter from Chet, the sorrow for both men, the return of her anguish…yeah, it had been stressful for her. And she was sure, given his problems and the fact that he had to be grieving, too, for Chet and for his own lost life, as well as facing his deficits again and again, that he might well be reaching his limits, too.

It was time for some rest. Some relaxation. Some iced tea on the front porch as the last of the long twilight faded away to reveal a diamond-studded night sky.

"Did you settle in okay?"

"I guess."

Something about that made her head upstairs as soon as the table was cleared. Looking at the guest room, she saw he hadn't settled in at all. His full backpack lay on the floor. The sheets and blankets she kept folded on the mattress hadn't been touched. He had neither unpacked nor made up his bed.

She heard him climb the steps and come to stand behind her. She didn't ask this time; she simply stepped in.

"Let's get this bed made," she said brightly. "I'll bet you didn't see a single fitted sheet the entire time you were in service."

He helped open the bottom sheet, and as soon as she fit the pocket around one corner, he grasped the sheet and took care of the rest. He didn't want to unpack, though. As soon as she suggested it, he simply shook his head. She wondered if he was expecting to be sent on his way soon. That caused her another pang.

Okay, she thought. He could learn swiftly. That was good news. She imagined there were a lot of things he hadn't needed to do since his injury, that his rehab had focused on giving him just enough skills to put him out the door. All too often, she had heard, vets were getting far less care than they needed.

Later, after a quiet few hours on the porch and then in front of a TV movie she hardly saw but that seemed to appeal to him, she stretched out in bed and stared up at the ceiling.

How many deficits did he have? How qualified was she to help him with them? Research was going to be necessary, but surely she could help him through that damn diagram tomorrow and they'd both learn something. She'd be the first to admit there were a whole lot of things she didn't know how to do or couldn't do herself.

He was in the same position, but at a different end of the scale. With his reading, for example. She was qualified to teach reading. From there…well, hadn't he said something about needing lists? She could make simple lists for him. Evidently, he could read some, but probably wasn't ready to take on an entire book. Maybe he never would be, but some reading was necessary to getting by, although she had known a guy once who couldn't read at all. He had managed by dint of a quick intelligence.

But this was a bigger deal than not being able to read. Her mind spun with all she had gathered today, and with ideas about what they might be able to do about at least some of it.

One thing for sure, she wasn't going to leave him to the mercies of the empty road and a world that wouldn't understand.

She owed it to Chet. Hell, she owed it to Liam. And she owed it to herself.

In his own bed, Liam couldn't sleep. Sleep often eluded him because it gave him too much empty time. The docs hadn't been sure whether the insomnia had been caused by his injury, or by his anxiety about his injury.

In fact, one thing he'd learned in rehab was that this whole TBI business was a bit of a mystery, even to the people trying to treat it. There was a cluster of symptoms that seemed to affect most patients, but the doctors weren't sure all of them had a physical basis. There was emotional fallout, too, but again, they couldn't say how much was brain damage and how much arose from the stress and frustration of dealing with that damage.

He'd have liked to know. He honestly wished he knew how much was permanent, how much would improve and how much simply arose from the situation. Knowing that would have helped him deal with it.

But nobody had certain answers. Apparently, from what one doc had said, having an estimated quarter million vets with TBI was taxing their limited knowledge. People were now surviving injuries that once would have killed them.

Thank you, Kevlar.

He touched the side of his head where he could still feel the scar. He'd discovered he was lucky to have that injury. A lot of guys with no outward injury at all were suffering from the same thing with nothing to prove it. If you didn't have an injury, but had concussive TBI, you were apt to be dismissed as having post-traumatic stress disorder. Like that was somehow less important.

Damn, the frustration was building in him again. He tossed on the bed, tried to quiet his mind and failed.

There'd been times when he'd felt exactly like a guinea pig. Try this, try that, let's see what works. He'd actually been glad when they'd judged him fit enough to be sent back to the world.

Which basically meant he could put a lid on his temper and function passably enough in society, at least superficially. He was a success story, a box checked off on someone's list somewhere. Come back in a year for a follow-up.

He could, if he wanted to, get bitter. But he apparently wasn't the type. He did, however, get royally frustrated. Remembering who he had been and comparing it to who he was now made it hard to control his temper sometimes.

He wasn't sure about this arrangement with Sharon, either. How long would she be able to put up with him?

Would he leave here in a couple of days feeling worse about himself?

It was possible, and the thought of that was almost enough to make him get up, grab his pack and hit the road again. He wasn't in the best shape for dealing with new problems.

He hated admitting that to himself. Recognizing limitations like this was new to him, and it didn't fit with who he felt he should be. Damn, he used to lead men in battle. As a senior NCO, he used to organize his squad's operations. He used to do a lot of stuff he didn't think he could do anymore.

Now here he was depending on a widow's charity. That made him feel small. But then he remembered the teasing way she'd poked his biceps and said she needed his physical strength.

Yeah, she probably did. She was strong in a lot of ways, of that he was certain, but she was still a bit of a mite, size-wise, and probably could use some muscle around here.

That made him feel a bit better. He'd just see how it went. That was pretty much the way he had to live now: see how it went.

It might go okay, and he owed that woman something because she was his best friend's widow.

Tired of struggling for sleep, he rose and walked to the window, looking out at the moonless night. This wasn't how he and Chet had talked about him visiting here when they could set it up. No, it had been the two of them and the promise of a great time, drinking a few beers, helping build that castle in the air, fooling around.

He'd imagined them walking around the ranch together while Chet showed him everything he'd been talking about. He'd imagined helping paint and put up wallpaper and fixing the front-porch railing Chet insisted was too loose.

The front-porch railing. Suddenly, he remembered those posts in the barn. Maybe that w-s what they were for. He'd ask Sharon tomorrow.

For the first time in a long time, he had his own plans for the morning: fixing a door and figuring out the porch-rail problem.

That felt good, too. And while he stayed at the window sleepless for a long time, neither the anxiety nor the frustration returned.

He had a plan.

Chapter Three

The morning dawned dismally, with a heavily pregnant gray sky and occasional spits of rain. Sharon showered and dressed, then headed downstairs. She was surprised to find Liam was already up, bent over the door frame diagram. He looked up, the furrows in his brow fading into a small smile as he saw her.

"Getting anywhere?" she asked.

"Maybe."

"Yeah, that was my feeling, too, when I looked at it last night. You're looking at someone who has trouble following directions for putting together a piece of pre-made furniture."

"Really? You're not just saying that?" For an instant, his light green eyes looked suspicious.

"No, I'm not just saying that. Chet teased me mercilessly about it. My excuse is that women aren't as good as men with spatial perception. I finally got so I could do better without following directions."

A chuckle escaped him. He waved the printout. "This is as bad as a puzzle."

"I'm lousy at them, too. Bring it out to the kitchen and we'll try to sort it out while I make breakfast. Bacon and eggs?"

She made coffee first, then they sat with mugs at the tile-topped table and pored over the diagram while bacon sizzled. Finally, Sharon jumped up. "I'm going to get a highlighter. Maybe we can ignore the stuff we don't need better that way."

She didn't tell him she had figured it out. She just wondered how much more damage they were going to do by tearing out the old wood. Ah, well. They did, after all, have directions for building a whole new frame, if necessary.

When she returned, he surprised her by taking the highlighter from her. "All we need to do is remove the strip I split." He put his finger on the piece on the drawing, then sat back studying it.

She let him take the lead, rising from time to time to put on some fresh bacon. She made a lot of bacon because he looked like a man with a large appetite. "Eggs?" she asked.

"Three, please."

Yup, big appetite.

But the really important thing was what she saw unfolding at the table.

"You got a different color of these?" he asked, holding up the highlighter.

"Dozens. Let me get them."

"A pen, too," he said.

She hurried to her office and returned with a box of fluorescent highlighters and a pen and pencil.

"Okay," he said. "Can you write the key? All I want is an order based on the colors."

"I can do that." She grabbed a magnetic pad from the refrigerator and watched while she kept an eye on the eggs.

"Check me if you think I'm wrong," he said, then started by highlighting the piece they needed to remove.

"That's number one. Yellow."

She wrote that on the pad. The process continued slowly as they ate their breakfasts and drank more coffee, but she felt a huge pleasure that she didn't have to step in. He was indeed figuring it out on his own. Bit by bit, he highlighted different actions in the exploded diagram until he had them all.

"Except," he said as he reached for the last piece of toast, "we have to do part of this in reverse."

"Remove that one piece, you mean?"

His eyes were smiling as he looked at her. "Yup." His sense of achievement was almost palpable.

She leaned over, studying the diagram and comparing it to the key. "That's not too hard."

"It shouldn't be."

"Except for pulling out that piece. If I get a pry bar we're apt to make a bigger problem."

"True." He frowned in thought as he chewed. "Something so simple shouldn't be so difficult."

It almost sounded as if he were talking to himself, so she didn't answer. As it was, given how he had spoken about himself, she was pretty impressed by how he had worked out the problem.

"Fix the door," he said, this time clearly to himself.

He was helping himself to focus, she supposed, given what he had said yesterday about talking to himself so he wouldn't lose track of what he was doing. She couldn't imagine what that must be like. Well, on second thought, maybe she could. How many times had she walked around looking for a pair of scissors while thinking about something else, ensuring she didn't forget what she wanted by making a scissoring movement with her fingers. Maybe that could be like what he was doing, only he had to do it more often.

"Finishing nails," he said, looking at the diagram and stabbing his finger at the tiny nails. "It must be attached by finishing nails. Painted over so we can't see them. They shouldn't be hard to pull. We just have to be gentle."

Then he beamed at her, problem solved. "I can do this."

So she let him.

She just walked to the back of the house, saying she had some bills to pay, and left him standing there. Left him to complete the job on his own, as if she believed he could do it. He would have felt a whole lot better if he'd believed that himself.

Beside the doorjamb, tacked to the wall were the diagram and the key. The key was an especially important reminder, and he suspected she had written in clear block letters only to make it easier on him.

But now the anxiety crept back in, a load of self-doubt badgered him and mocked him. For so long now he'd been learning what he couldn't do, and learning actually very little of what he might be able to do, especially with some practice. He'd been diminished in part by the trauma, and in part by all the lessons and warnings thrust at him.

In response to the anxiety, anger lit a short fuse and he had to clamp down on it. He hated this. He hated living with constant doubts and uncertainty. He didn't so much mind failing at something as he did fearing that he might.

It sometimes made him want to smash his fist into a wall.

But smashing a wall would only frighten Sharon, would only make another job for him to solve and it wouldn't fix the damn door he was staring at.

He'd figured out the diagram, which had looked like so much spaghetti at first. If he could do that, he could follow through on the job.

Just do it.

That voice came from the past, from a time when matters of life and death had been staring at him in the face. *Just do it. Quit being a coward.*

He'd never been a coward. Afraid, sure, but a coward? No. That word spurred him as few others could have, and he reached for the pry bar and the piece of wood he was going to use to spread the pressure to avoid damaging more of the door frame.

He could do this. He just had to believe it.

In the end, with the directions to follow, it turned out to be easy. He just kept moving one step at a time. And with each step, he felt a whole lot better.

Sharon sat in her office with a textbook open in front of her, one she hadn't had a need to review in a while. It provided a decent overview for recognizing cognitive impairment and working with it. Of course it was designed for teachers dealing with students, and for all she knew, this could be a very different situation.

The book led her to some further research on the web and she spent more than she probably should have buying copies of relevant journal articles.

She had no delusions that she would be able to help much. Liam's situation was far beyond the scope of her training and experience. But at least she could have some idea of what they were dealing with here, and maybe the things to avoid, if nothing else.

And all the while she was reading, at the back of her mind she was waiting for the cussing to begin. Chet used to say a man couldn't do a job without a little colorful language. She'd grown used to the air turning blue around him when something didn't go right, and she expected to hear at least some of it from Liam.

She heard none, and that began to trouble her. Had he just walked out, unable to deal with the door and angry at himself? Or worse, feeling like a failure?

But every time she nearly jumped up to go out there, she'd hear another bang, or the sound of some tool, and would settle back into her chair. She had told him to let her know if he needed anything.

Looking out the window across the yard between the house and the barn, she saw that the sky outside was turning even darker. A storm was brewing. Good. They needed the rain desperately.

Inevitably, she remembered how much she and Chet had loved to sit on the porch when a storm approached, feeling the breeze stiffen and the air cool while thunder marched steadily closer. The wildness of storms had always appealed to her, and thinking about those lazy afternoons with Chet felt bittersweet. Good memories, gone too soon.

She sighed, leaning her chin on her elbow, and just let her mind wander. So often she simply tried to avoid remembering because that was the best way to avoid the pain. But with time, the quality of her grief had changed. Yesterday when Liam had arrived, Pandora's Box had opened, and the grief had been fresh, excruciating and very real.

Today, though, it had gentled, allowing her to remember the good things, not just the loss. She didn't want to lose those good memories, and given that Chet had been away so much during their marriage, there weren't exactly a whole lot of them. Once she had actually counted how many days they had been together since their wedding, actually together, and seven years of marriage had totaled up to less than an entire year of days.

They'd had Skype, they'd written countless emails, even had quite a few phone calls, but in the end they'd shared the same space for such a small amount of time that she found it hard to believe. Painful, too. They'd spent so much time looking forward, planning for when they could always be together, she wondered if they hadn't missed some of the "now."

But how could she really say that? Dreams were the fuel of life, and how they had dreamed. Lots and lots of shared dreams.

"I finished."

Liam's voice startled her out of her reverie and she jumped. How had she not heard him approach?

"Sorry," he said. "Didn't mean to scare you."

"It's okay. Just lost in thought. Did you say you were done. Already?"

He shrugged. "I think it's been a couple of hours. Come look. If you don't like it, I can maybe do something."

She glanced at the time on her computer and realized he was right. The morning was nearly gone. A loud rumble of thunder finished waking her from her preoccupation. "Sounds like it's going to get bad," she remarked.

He nodded, then stood back to clear the doorway for her. She walked ahead of him to the front door and stood there in amazement. She wasn't sure what she had expected but it was not an absolutely perfect repair job. All it needed now was paint. He'd even put the hook back.

"Wow!" She turned to him with a grin. "That's a beautiful job! Why wouldn't I like it?"

He kind of tipped his head, almost as if to say he didn't know. Maybe he felt he couldn't judge it. Maybe the cancer of uncertainty was just eating him alive. That troubled her, especially after the way he'd burst into her life, seeming so determined and so frank about his problems.

But then she remembered from her research that people with TBI often experienced mood swings. Yesterday he'd been bursting with energy. Today he just seemed tired.

She looked at the door again, at the diagrams beside it, and considered how taxing it might have all been for him. How would she know?

A crack of thunder shook the house. He winced and reminded her that he had more than one trauma behind him. Loud noises were probably uncomfortable for him. They had become so for Chet.

"Let's celebrate," she said impulsively.

"Celebrate?"

"Sure. You fixed my door and you did it perfectly. I couldn't have done that."

"Don't patronize me." His response was almost sharp, but not quite.

Stymied, surprised, her mouth opened a bit. Then she shook her head. "I wasn't patronizing you, I was complimenting you. And I'm quite serious. I don't think I could have done it. My deep, dark secret is that I'm not handy at all. Let's go make some cocoa. From the sound of that thunder, it's about to get chilly."

Without another word, she headed for the kitchen, discomfort gnawing at her. Had she made a mistake inviting this man to stay? Was he that unpredictable, that sensitive? A ticking emotional time bomb?

It really sank home then that she was out of her depth, and that Chet's best friend might not be at all the same man anymore.

How could she have failed to consider that? God, she felt like an idiot.

But even as she began to pull things out of the cupboard and the refrigerator, one certainty stayed with her: she wasn't going to be the one to throw this man out, back on an empty road with no place to go.

She was already heating and stirring the cocoa on the stove when she heard him limp into the kitchen.

"Sorry," he said. "I told you I have a temper problem."

"If that was temper, it's nothing. Seriously, I wasn't

patronizing you. I was truly impressed." She didn't look up from the pot.

"Thank you. That's the correct answer, right?"

She looked at him at last. "Sit down. Cocoa will be ready in a minute. Then we can talk and maybe figure out how to get along."

"If I'm causing a problem..."

She wasn't going to stand for that. "Cut it out. I said we'll talk. Unless you're in a rush to hit the road again."

This time he didn't say a thing, just pulled a chair out and sat.

Okay, this was going to be an interesting experience. Having a total stranger in the house would be enough by itself, but one whose reactions were a little unpredictable might be something else.

She closed her eyes a moment before lifting the pot from the stove and pouring cocoa into two mugs. Chet, she reminded herself, would want her to do this. More, she was beginning to realize that she needed to do it for herself. It might make her feel like something more than an automaton, a biological machine that moved through the days too often on autopilot.

Since Chet's death, she had avoided any real emotional investment. Even with her students. She still did all the right things; she still cared about them, but not with the same depth. In short, she had become a bit crippled. Maybe it was time to deal with her own issues, too.

She joined Liam at the table, putting one mug in front of him. "It's hot," she said automatically.

He nodded and wrapped his big hands around the cup. Another crack of thunder resounded, loud and hollow, rolling across the sky. This time Liam didn't wince, but his eyes darted a bit nervously.

"Tell me about your rehab," she said, figuring a distraction might be wise.

"What about it?"

"Well, I don't *know* anything about it, so I'd like to hear. Didn't Chet tell you I'm as curious as a cat?"

That brought a faint smile to his lips, and he seemed to relax at last. He sipped cocoa. "That's a big subject."

"So start wherever. Did you think it was good?"

"It was probably better than a lot of guys got. Mainly because I was so messed up. They either had to help me with the basics or keep me in a hospital forever."

She parsed that into separate topics. "Messed up? How bad?"

"I was like a freaking baby in a lot of ways. I couldn't remember whole, big patches of my life, I couldn't feed myself, I couldn't walk. It was like a lot of stuff just got erased." He patted his leg. "This one is still trying to remember. They said it should, eventually."

"But you got back your memory?"

"Most of it, I think. I'm not aware of too many holes, but if I can't remember, how would I know?"

There was suddenly a sparkle in his unusual eyes, and she gathered he was trying to joke. She gave him a laugh. "Good question."

"Basically, I remember enough to know who I am and who I was."

That hit her, causing another pang. "That's hard, isn't it?"

"Yeah. I know I used to be able to do stuff, but damned if I can figure out how to do it now. It's weird. Like the door. I knew I should know what to do about it, but I couldn't remember *how.*"

She nodded, trying to imagine it and failing. "God, that must be frustrating."

He didn't deny it. "So anyway, my memory started mending. They taught me how to do the basics physically, and they put me through some therapy to deal with the frustration and anger. Then when they felt I could control my outbursts and take care of my basic needs, I was discharged."

"That's it?"

"What more could they do?"

"What about learning to read and write again, little things like that?" She was beginning to feel angry.

"Sharon…" He hesitated. "They don't have the time or resources to teach everyone everything. There are too many of us. And some don't even get as much help as I did."

She didn't want to know why. At that moment she felt angry enough to explode.

"Are you going to go ballistic?" he asked.

"I'm trying not to."

"Chet said you have a temper."

"I do," she admitted. "Some things just make me livid. So how were you supposed to get by? Just tell me that."

"I could walk and talk and behave reasonably well. It could be worse."

Of course it could. But it was a small leap from thinking about his case to thinking about how she would have felt if Chet had been the one sitting across the table from her telling her this.

"Not even any job training?"

"Once I decide where I want to stay, I can probably find a local group to help with that."

"Oh. Really." And how was he supposed to decide where to stay? Damn, she just couldn't imagine it. How many others were there like him—thrown out of care and onto the mercy of friends and families or even strangers, without some of the most basic skills? Another loud rumble of thunder shook the house, and she dimly heard the rain begin to fall. She hoped it would be a good soaker.

But she needed to stop asking questions right now, for both their sakes. This couldn't be comfortable for him, and it was certainly infuriating her. Let it go for now, she told herself. Take it minute by minute.

She drew a deep breath to calm herself, and tried to sip cocoa as if everything were ordinary and normal. Racking her brain, she came up with something positive to say. "You know what I bet? I bet you remember more than you've had an opportunity to find out. I mean, you've been out of rehab only a short time, but you navigated your way here. There are probably a lot of things still there that you just haven't called on yet."

"Maybe." He smiled faintly. "Chet also said you were an optimist."

"It serves me well. But think about it. You were the one who came up with the idea of simplifying that diagram with a bunch of different colors and a key. I'd bet there are bunches of stuff you just haven't had time to run into that you can still do."

He thought about it. "I hope so. I guess I'm going to find out."

"I'm almost positive I'm right. Rehab is basically a sterile environment. You do certain things, learn certain things. And there's a whole bunch of other stuff you never encounter. I think you're in for some pleasant surprises."

His smile widened. "I can see why Chet loved you."

She froze, astounded but not offended. Then he cussed.

"I told you I just say whatever comes into my head sometimes. Sorry."

He started to push back from the table, but she shot out her hand and stopped him. "Don't. I was just... surprised. You talk about Chet so easily. None of my friends do. They try not to mention him at all anymore."

"They're afraid of hurting you."

"It hurts more to act like he never existed. That was a nice thing to say."

"So it's okay if I talk about him?"

"Absolutely. We both loved him. And that gives me a thought. How would you feel about meeting some of his friends from around here? Not immediately, but when you feel more settled in."

He ruminated a few moments. "Maybe. I'll think about it."

She realized she still gripped his forearm and forced herself to let go. But in that moment of awareness, she felt something deeper, something exciting. Something she hadn't felt in way too long.

Be careful, she warned herself, even as heat tried to pool between her thighs. She'd been alone too long, and while she didn't especially want her sexual urges to reawaken, she could understand why they might. They might also get her into a lot of trouble.

Damn, she was sitting here across from a virtual stranger, feeling longings that had once been utterly reserved for Chet. She didn't think he'd blame her for that, but she felt guilty, anyway. Chet's best friend? Oh, man, that didn't seem right.

"Sharon? Something wrong?"

Whatever else he'd lost, he hadn't lost his ability to read people. Or maybe she was just the open book some people claimed she was. Sometimes her friends teased her that every thought in her head was written on her face.

There were advantages to that, though. She almost smiled as she thought of the way her students always seemed to realize when they were pushing her too far, or annoying her, without her saying a word.

"I'm fine," she lied, hoping he believed her, hoping the thought of her students calmed her expression. Apparently it did because he relaxed.

Another rumble of loud thunder rattled the window, and rain began to fall in earnest. Sharon realized the room had grown dark, and she rose to turn on a light.

It revealed a handsome man who was staring down into his mug as if he might find answers there. Then he said something that took them in a totally different direction. "Chet really wanted to keep wolves?"

"I don't think we could," she admitted. "Wolves often travel fifty miles in a day. I think they'd go nuts enclosed in a space as small as ours."

"Maybe." He stood up abruptly. "I need to get busy with something. A walk doesn't seem like a good idea."

"Doing anything outdoors doesn't seem like a good idea right now," she agreed. She wondered if he needed physical activity or just something to occupy him. For all she knew, he was trying to straighten out something in his head, or just answer a need. No way to know. "Any ideas? With the weather, I'm kind of stymied."

"Plans," he said. "I need a plan."

"In what way?"

"I need a list. I need to know that I've got something to do."

She bit her lip, hesitating, uncertain.

Then he spoke with painful honesty. "I've got to be occupied. I need to know that the next hours aren't empty. I need to focus. It keeps me from building a head of steam. Anything you want done?"

So keeping busy helped him stay level. She understood that perfectly. In the months after Chet died, the only thing that had saved her had been keeping busy. At times she had become almost frenetic with activity. Sometimes she still did.

"You want a long list or just a single task?" she asked.

"A list would be better, but a task will do for starters."

"Let me think a minute. There's a lot of stuff that needs doing outside, but inside not so much."

He cocked his eyes toward the window. "It looks dark as night out there."

It was a good storm, all right. The windows rattled again, and this time the thunder seemed to rumble through the ground, as well. She watched him and saw the inevitable tightening at the sound. She'd seen Chet react the same way and wondered if vets ever got so they could stand certain types of sounds again.

"The dryer hose needs cleaning," she said, calling him back just as he seemed about to be going elsewhere in his mind. "I hate that job, and it's been too long."

"That's a start. I'm pretty sure I can manage that. Anything else?"

"I'll be thinking."

One corner of his mouth lifted. "You do that."

But she wondered what she was going to come up with. All her own frenetic activity had pretty well kept the interior of this place in top shape. White-glove inspection shape. Plenty of compulsion had driven her.

But at least now she had a way to connect with what Liam was experiencing, and that felt like a major step.

Chapter Four

Sleep was still hard to come by, but the harder Sharon worked Liam, the easier it was for him to find. It also helped that he *did* know how to do some things, like painting.

Two days after the storm, when she had announced she needed to go to town to buy exterior paint for the house and barn, he almost didn't go with her. He still found groups of strangers to be threatening, but he told himself to get the hell over it. He wasn't at war any longer, and God willing, he never would be again. Besides, it seemed downright asinine and ungentlemanly to let her go to town and pick up all that heavy paint alone. If he was good for anything at all anymore, he'd make a damn fine beast of burden.

So he clenched his teeth and climbed into the pickup

cab with her. Back to civilization. Damn it, he'd done harder things.

She smiled as he joined her in the truck and put it into gear. "If you start to feel like it's too much, let me know. There's nothing on my list that can't wait. Or you can stay in the truck."

"You don't have to coddle me."

He realized he was doing it again— snapping at people who were just trying to be nice. Damn it. That was one of the most annoying things about his new self. He opened his mouth to apologize, but she forestalled him.

"I'm not coddling you," she retorted just as sharply. "I'm just letting you know it's okay with me if I can't finish everything today. Just being polite."

Yup, just being polite. Something he seemed to have forgotten. He could feel her simmering beside him as they jolted down her long driveway and then onto the pavement of the road into Conard City.

"I know I'm not easy," he said finally. "If you want, just drop me out here and I'll walk back."

"Did I say that? Did I even suggest that? The thing is, Liam, at some point you have to understand that I have a temper, too. You're damn well not alone in that, and I'm going to snap at you as often as you snap at me. I'm not perfect, so why should you be?"

Good question. He watched the rangeland roll by, the mountains slowly shrinking into the background.

"Do you still want to do the painting?" she asked.

"Hell, yes. I said I would." He'd paint every inch of her ranch including the fields if she wanted because getting back on the road with nowhere to go didn't make sense, and because he felt he owed it to Chet. And because he needed the work she was giving him.

And not least of all because he needed not to be alone. She kept him from being alone. When the noise inside his skull got too loud, he could count on her to drown it out with some conversation.

It was a dependency. He didn't like it, but there it was. But then, when had he ever really been independent? Hadn't he always relied on his buddies?

And where were these questions coming from? Maybe he was getting back some of his brain power, actually thinking about something besides self-control.

He glanced at Sharon, who was staring down the road. "Are you still mad at me?"

"No. I may erupt, but staying mad is a waste of time and energy."

She didn't sound angry and even flashed a smile his way.

"Chet liked your temper," he told her.

"He said that?"

"Yeah. He said he never had to wonder if you were upset or about what." He watched another smile dawn on her face and felt relieved that he hadn't put his foot in it again. Maybe he'd get the hang of this conversation business, after all. Eventually. "But he also said you never really blew up."

"Not often." She bit her lip. "Did he talk about me a lot?"

He realized that she must be thirsty to know about the times when he was away from her, the places she couldn't share with him. Even now. Maybe especially now, because he'd never come back to tell her himself.

"Often enough, when we'd be sitting somewhere all alone. Especially when it was dark. Times like that, I knew I had to pay extra attention."

"How come?"

"Because his mind would be back here with you. Somebody had to keep an eye out. But I enjoyed listening."

"You must have been bored, really."

"If I was, I don't remember it. He was really crazy about you. I think he'd want you to know that."

"Thank you."

He almost sighed with relief. Okay, he'd done it right. Of course, he was telling the simple truth, but at least he hadn't managed to put his foot in it somehow.

It struck him then that he'd arrived here just a few days ago like the loose end in somebody else's life, but he wasn't feeling quite so much like a loose end anymore. He felt an unfamiliar smile stretch his face.

"Something funny?" she asked.

"No. I'm just feeling good." He savored the feeling, and hoped it wouldn't disappear the instant they got to town.

Then she said something that let him know he'd gone and said exactly the wrong thing again.

"When…when Chet was shot, he, um, wasn't distracted, was he?"

"Distracted?" Then he made the connection with what he'd said about how he had to pay more attention when Chet was talking about her. He cussed himself. "Hell, no! We were in a firefight. He wasn't thinking about anything except that."

"Okay."

He hesitated, trying to find words, but as they sometimes did, they slipped away like eels. All he knew was that he had to find a way to make her feel better. "He wasn't careless, Sharon." Did that make enough sense?

He wasn't sure. "He wanted to come home. He wanted all of us to come home."

She nodded without taking her eyes from the road. Was he imagining it, or did she seem tenser? Tighter? "Did he... Did he say anything?"

Oh, crap. "Last words? No. He didn't have time. It was that fast."

"Thank God!"

Her reaction, and the vehemence of it, startled him. It was his turn to stare down the road and try to put the pieces together. He guessed she was just glad it had been quick. Well, he could understand that. Not everyone was so lucky, especially in the days of body armor. He just hoped she didn't ask for details.

The next ten minutes passed in a chasm of silence he didn't know how to cross. He could only imagine what roads her mind might be traveling, and he feared the roads he might follow in his own thoughts. Not because they were unfamiliar to him, but because they were so damn upsetting at times. Taking a trip back to some of the worst experiences of his life didn't seem like a smart thing to do. On the other hand, worrying about some kind of future he couldn't even begin to envision didn't seem a whole lot better.

He felt like he was in...what was the word? Limbo? Wait, wasn't that a dance? He hated the way a word could do that to him, leaving him uncertain as to whether he understood it. He tried again. He felt like he was in...a no-man's-land. That worked.

Trapped in a moment. A little section of time. He knew there was a past to it, and he vaguely remembered that he'd once had ideas about a future, but right now it was all dim and sometimes even felt as if it belonged to someone else.

The houses were starting to show up more frequently, many of them closer to the road. They were approaching town now and a new kind of tension began to build in him. He wondered if populated areas would always cause him problems, although it seemed kind of ridiculous to him when he thought how some of the worst troubles he'd encountered had been in seemingly isolated mountains.

He glanced in the side mirror and saw the mountains, still receding behind him, and wondered if he shouldn't take the bull by the horns and hike up there. He was certainly going to have to take the whole town thing by the horns. Repeatedly.

As the traffic grew a little heavier, so did his state of wariness. It wasn't as bad as it had been, though. Not nearly. He drew the deep breaths they'd taught him and settled down. He hardly noticed the charm, or lack of it, as they passed through the center of Conard City, because he was focused on staying calm.

Ridiculous, he told himself. There was absolutely nothing about this place that should rake up any memories or bad reactions. It had to be the closed-in feeling.

At last, Sharon turned them onto a large gravel parking lot outside a huge lumberyard. Hambley's Lumber, for Home and Ranch, a large sign said. The sign looked weathered, and a small corner was missing. He had to make himself walk beside Sharon into the interior, but a sense of ease overcame him unexpectedly as he smelled fresh wood. It was as if the smell took him back to a good time, and he was able to relax a bit and look around, taking things in.

Sharon made a beeline, evidently knowing exactly where she wanted to go. He noted the way she smiled and said hello to everyone they passed, as if she knew them all. And maybe she did. That increased his comfort level even more.

He saw the paint counter just ahead, but before they arrived, Sharon was stopped by a tall man of about thirty-five, wearing a green bib apron over jeans and a checked shirt. The apron was stamped "Hambley's" on the front.

"Sharon, it's been a while."

"Ed! How nice to see you." She gave the man a brief hug. "I'm just here to buy paint and supplies. Lots of paint."

"Gonna red the place up, huh?"

"That's the plan."

Then the man's dark eyes tracked to Liam. "Got yourself a handyman?"

"Actually," Sharon said, turning to Liam with a smile and extending her hand to encourage him to come closer, "this is Liam O'Connor, Chet's army buddy. He's been kind enough to offer to help me."

The response was instantaneous. Ed looked at him, then looked at Sharon and there was no mistaking the shopkeeper was attracted to her. Liam's response was equally swift. He felt a surge of protectiveness toward Sharon. Maybe even possessiveness.

The strength of the feeling took him by surprise, and he tried to rein it in, even as he reached out to shake Ed's hand. He had no right to feel possessive or even protective about Sharon. No right at all. But as he met Ed's smile, he recognized the competitiveness there.

Ed had his eye on Chet's widow and didn't like a

stranger moving in, especially one with ties to Chet. Some instincts were primal enough that not even a TBI could erase them completely.

Then he stomped down on that train of thought, asking himself how he could be sure he wasn't just imagining it all. Uncertainty was his constant companion these days.

Ed turned back to Sharon. "So what are you painting?"

"House and barn. You'll have to help me estimate how much paint I need."

"And you're the teacher," Ed said with a wink.

"There's awfully dry wood in some places," Sharon retorted with a laugh. "Rough, too."

Ed put his hand on Sharon's shoulder and guided her to the paint counter. "There are easy ways to handle this."

Liam clamped his jaw, irritated by the familiar way Ed touched Sharon. He took another deep breath and tried to plaster a pleasant smile on his face, reminding himself he had no claim whatever on this woman.

"Pick your colors," Ed was saying. "But you don't want to pick up too much of it today because it'll start separating. What I can do, though, is make a delivery every time you need more. No need for you to take it all at once, or cart it out there yourself."

"I have help," Sharon said, flashing a smile at Liam. "But I can see what you mean about the paint separating, and stirring it is no fun."

Stirring paint might be just the kind of activity Liam needed, but he didn't say so. Painting would keep him even busier.

"Well, then, which do you want to start with and what color?"

Sharon looked at Liam. "House or barn?"

She was asking him to decide? He'd gotten used to making very few decisions since his injury, but now he wondered if that was mostly because he hadn't been allowed to or because he couldn't. Either way, it was on him to answer, and hesitating too long might make him look stupid to Ed. "Barn," he said decisively, though he was far from feeling decisive.

"I agree," Sharon answered promptly. "It needs it more than the house."

"I'd suggest staining," Ed said, "but as I recall, there's still some old paint on the place. The wood's pretty weathered, though. It's going to be thirsty."

Gallons of primer headed the list. "This," Sharon said, "is what I get for neglecting it for so long."

"You could have called me. I'd have brought the boys out."

Liam felt again that powerful surge of possessive protectiveness. God, he needed to put a damper on this. It probably qualified right alongside the anger they'd helped him work on. Unwanted, and potentially dangerous.

"Thanks, Ed," Sharon answered, "but there was a plan in place. That kind of…changed."

Changed? A nice way of putting Chet's death. Liam felt the whisper of old grief, for himself and Sharon.

Once the order was placed, Liam carried several gallons of primer out to the truck while Ed followed with painting tools and a heap of rags.

Ed lingered at the truck, though. "You need help,

holler," he said. This time he addressed his words to Liam. "It's a lot for one man."

"Thanks," Liam managed. He hoped he sounded pleasant.

At last, they climbed into the truck, and Ed headed back to his business.

"He's such a nice man," Sharon remarked.

"Yes."

"Something wrong?"

"Not a thing." He felt her eyes on him but refused to return her gaze. The things going on inside him weren't for sharing. Then he wondered if they were rational. But why should they be? They were *feelings*.

"Hell," he muttered.

"What?"

"Just getting tangled in my own head again. Yes, Ed seemed nice."

"I was going to offer you lunch at Maude's diner. But it's small and usually crowded."

He bridled a bit, even as he realized it might be a difficult time for him. But going to a diner? He took the bit between his teeth. "Sure, that sounds great. My treat."

The only way he was going to emerge from this tunnel he'd been staggering his way through for so long now was to punch a hole in the side and fight his way out of it. The image pleased him enough to put a smile on his face. He could do this.

Sharon acutely sensed the ebb and flow of whatever was going on inside Liam. She couldn't ascribe it to particular things, but she felt it, anyway—the moments of tension, the instants of irritation, the seconds of uncertainty. He was on quite a roller coaster during this trip to town, and she wondered if it was good for him to do all this or if it might give him problems.

But he was the one who said he wanted to go to the diner, and with only the merest hesitation on the doorstep, he plunged in.

She couldn't help but wonder what it must feel like to be a man who could remember facing the most god-awful thing in the world, namely war, and then find yourself unwilling to face a crowded diner.

Why should that be? What exactly had happened to him? Or perhaps the self-doubt had crept in while he was recovering his physical skills and learning to control his temper.

Given that he had warned her he often said things he shouldn't, she thought he'd done remarkably well at the paint store, especially with Ed acting like there was no way Liam could do this job alone. Maybe he couldn't but that should be his decision, not Ed's.

As it was a weekday, and still a bit early for lunch, the diner wasn't overly crowded. It was only as they slid into a booth that Sharon realized she might have made a huge mistake. Maude had a tendency to slam things around, seem angry at her customers most of the time and speak sharply. Sharon didn't know if Liam was ready for the full treatment.

"Maybe we shouldn't eat here," she said.

"Why?"

"Maude."

"Who's Maude?"

"She owns the place. Chet used to say she was like a drill instructor. Liam, she's going to slam things down in front of you and be very sharp in her manner."

"Really?" To her amazement, Liam smiled. "Fore-warned is forearmed."

Now came Sharon's turn to tense up. She'd seen enough to know that Liam could control his temper decently, but he had never been exposed to Maude, who seemed to be anger personified. "She might not even let you order for yourself."

"You don't know how rarely I've ever been able to choose what I eat."

She hadn't thought about that. She guessed living off rations a lot of the time might make a person indifferent and willing to eat pretty much anything that wasn't freeze-dried and rehydrated.

And there was Maude, bearing down on them. Stocky, getting up in years, but as vital as ever, she stomped their way with a gleam in her dark eyes. It almost reminded Sharon of a cat that had spied a bird: predatory.

But Maude had a good heart. She just had the world's most unfortunate manner.

She reached their table and stared down at Liam. "Who's this?"

That was Maude, straight to the point. Before Liam could answer, Sharon said, "This is Liam. He was Chet's best buddy in the army."

"Took you long enough to get here."

Sharon nearly cringed. She wouldn't have blamed Liam for giving an equally sharp response. Instead, he surprised her.

"Some roads," he said, looking right at Maude, "are long and twisted."

Maude peered at him. "Maybe from Afghanistan they are." The response was monumentally unexpected from Maude, and evinced none of her usual antagonism. However, she still slapped the menus and the empty coffee mugs on the table in front of them. "Coffee?"

"Love some," Liam answered. Sharon managed a nod.

As soon as Maude had moved away out of earshot, Sharon leaned over and said quietly, "That was something. Maude's never that mellow."

Liam shrugged. "All you have to do is glare back."

How had she missed that? Had he really glared at Maude? Maybe so. Wow.

The notion made her want to giggle, and she quickly covered her mouth with her hand. She wouldn't want Maude to think she was being laughed at. Steaks had been burned for less.

"What do you recommend?" Liam asked.

Sharon remembered then that he might have trouble reading the menu. He had said he had could only read some, and menus could be daunting if they were packed, as Maude's was. Dang. He hadn't even reached for it. She wondered how she could broach the subject of teaching him.

"Well, Maude is famous for her steak sandwiches and pie."

"Then I'll have a steak sandwich."

By the time they were eating their sandwiches, Sharon was wondering what had gotten into Maude. Nothing got slammed in front of them at all. It was an amazing personality change, right down to a nicer tone of voice.

"You tamed the dragon," she told Liam as they climbed back into her truck.

"Not much of a dragon," he remarked. "I've met tougher ones."

"I'm serious. I've never seen her like that. Attitude comes with every meal at Maude's."

He laughed. "Maybe I'll see it next time."

She put the key in the ignition, then hesitated. "Liam?"

"Yeah?"

"Do you want to learn to read better? Because if you do, I can help. I *am* a teacher."

He was silent a few heartbeats. "They told me I might never be able to read much again. Not a book or anything like that. They weren't sure, but said in most cases like mine improvement might be limited. Something about where some of the damage is located."

"Oh." Her heart sank.

"On the other hand," he said, "I guess there's only one way to find out. Sure, let's give it a shot."

"I can go to the library and find early-reader books if you won't feel insulted. Or we can work out a method at home."

"Skip the library," he said after a moment. "I can read some things. Short things. It's not all gone."

"Then maybe you just need to brush up." Which was a hopeful statement indeed, she admitted to herself. Some things could never come back, depending on the degree and type of injury. She guessed they were going to explore some more of his limitations. She just hoped they didn't bring him to despair.

And that was how he came to be high on a ladder three days later, starting the second side of the barn, turning everything white with primer.

It was an easy, soothing job, one he had remembered well enough. It stole some of the constant tension he lived with, wondering when he was going to butt up hard against all that he'd lost. He could paint. That actually opened up possibilities for work in the future.

And the constant physical exertion relieved the anxiety that never quite left him. In fact, it banished it.

Up on that ladder, he actually felt as if everything was right in the world. As he was brushing and rolling his way over the weathered wood, he wondered if he should have taken Sharon's offer to rent the paint sprayer. He'd looked at it, decided he wasn't ready to test himself through *that,* and opted instead for brushes and rollers.

Truthfully, he didn't want this job to be easy. He needed the hard work, something sadly missing from his life for a while now, unless you counted rehab. Learning to walk and take care of himself had been labor all right. Hell, at one point getting a spoon from a bowl to his mouth had seemed overwhelming.

But things were looking up. Definitely. Now he had another tool in his pack to add to those he'd remastered.

Then there was reading. He wondered if he'd made it harder on Sharon by refusing the books, but he hadn't known how to tell her that the prospect of facing a book, even a children's book, had been rife with the potential for failure. The doctors had told him often enough that his reading skills might remain forever minimal, that he'd be fortunate if he could read even two pages in a book.

Sometimes he wondered if the doctors hadn't given him too many warnings. All for the best of reasons, of course. They'd prepared him for disappointments. Unfortunately, they'd also made him reluctant to try.

Well, that was going to change. He reached for the paint can hanging from a lower rung by a wire hook, and lifted it, refilling the roller pan. Yep, he was going to try some new things, just like he was working on reading.

He still knew the alphabet, which was good, and wasn't overwhelmed by single, common words. He recognized most of them on the flash cards Sharon had tested him with. Next was getting to sentences. Complexity. Putting words together correctly.

"Paint." He heard himself muttering the word and was recalled to the task at hand. Twenty feet high on a ladder didn't seem like a smart place to let his mind wander, and the muttering habit he'd developed brought him back once more.

That guy Ed had been right: this wood was soaking up paint like a desert would soak up water. He almost imagined he could hear it slurp.

He kind of liked the way some of the wood had silvered where the paint had been gone awhile, but he also remembered that wasn't good for the long run, so he remorselessly slapped primer over it.

He realized he had begun to spend a lot of time not thinking about Sharon. Deliberately avoiding thinking about her. He knew why, too. He'd come here carrying a letter to her from Chet, his best buddy ever, and the kinds of thoughts he kept having felt like a betrayal.

He'd reacted to his first view of her, of course. A very pretty woman, she undoubtedly drew many men's thoughts in sexual directions. But after this amount of time, he'd gotten used to how pretty she was. What he couldn't get used to was how strongly she attracted him. Damn, that just seemed to keep growing.

Anytime he came within a few feet of her, he smelled her, and she smelled good, especially the shampoo she used. He detected no other perfume, but she didn't need it. Her natural scents enticed him.

It had been a long time since he was attracted to a woman, and if he came right down to it, it would be even longer till he acted on that attraction, because he was afraid of his own bumbling. There were times in life when you really couldn't blurt out the wrong thing, or blurt something out the wrong way, and he seemed to possess an absolute genius for that these days. Keeping quiet and staying away from situations fraught with emotion seemed like the best course.

Glancing down, he saw he needed more paint. The pan was empty, the paint can hardly holding enough to fill a brush. Lifting the brush from where it dangled from another wire holder, he ran it around the inside of the paint can and swiped it against the wall repeatedly until it was nearly dry.

They were going to have to get Ed to deliver more soon. He didn't like that, and he knew exactly why.

"Selfish," he muttered to himself as he grabbed the can, pan, roller and brush and climbed down the ladder. "Damn fool," he added for good measure.

He didn't have a thing to offer a woman like Sharon, so why was some broken connection in his brain trying to put a fence around her? Sharon needed a whole man, not the dregs of one.

He had just reached the lowest rung of the ladder when he felt a prickle between his shoulder blades, the kind of prickle that had always warned him there were eyes on him.

The response was instinctive, so deeply ingrained that not even memory loss had killed it. In an instant, he crouched and began to scan the area.

Finally, he spied the intruder: little more than a dot in the distance, he saw a horse and rider coming this way. Admittedly, it was just a man on a horse, but in Afghanistan that hadn't always been innocent.

"Liam?"

At the sound of Sharon's voice, he spun around. She was carrying a pitcher of lemonade and a glass toward him.

"There's someone coming," he said tautly.

"Where?" Her brow furrowed and she looked around.

"Rider on the hill."

She looked where he pointed. "Relax," she said softly. "It's my neighbor, the guy who owns the sheep."

He looked at her, saw concern on her face, and realized he was being an idiot. The anger surged then, in response to feeling like a fool, but more probably in response to an adrenaline rush that had no outlet. He dropped the painting supplies on a tarp.

"I'm going for a walk." He strode away, ignoring her as she called his name. At one point in his life he'd seen enemies on every hill. Now he felt threatened by every approaching car.

Damn it. How was he supposed to live this way?

Chapter Five

Sharon watched Liam storm off across the field. She understood he needed to do it, but it broke her heart, anyway. That might have been Chet, and the thought was almost too much to bear.

At least when she'd glimpsed these reactions in Chet when he was home on leave, they hadn't been as strong, probably because when he came home he was in familiar surroundings and with familiar people. Liam didn't have that comfort. None of it.

He was a stranger in a strange land, a place so unfamiliar he couldn't adequately judge the threats. She hated to think of the overload he must sometimes feel on top of his cognitive deficits. Hell, people who came home with post-traumatic stress lived in a hell beyond imagining. How much worse must it be when you added all the TBI effects?

She was sure she hadn't begun to plumb the depths of all that Liam dealt with.

He'd seemed better the past few days but she didn't delude herself into thinking he was necessarily healing. He'd merely been occupied with an exhausting task. He'd said himself he needed to keep busy, and that part she understood. But there was no way she could truly grasp the rest of it. No way at all. She felt so inadequate.

She held the pitcher of lemonade in one hand, tucking the glass in her elbow so that she could wave to her neighbor. Then she turned and went back to the house, her mind spinning in a hundred different directions. There had to be more she could do. Something. Anything.

But she couldn't think of what it might be. The work wasn't enough, and that would run out, anyway. Then what? Clearly he needed some kind of anchor, some kind of secure point from which he could start taking his life back. The faster he painted, the more she feared for him. Was he going to finish and then take to the road again?

What then? Where would he go? What would he do?

She felt sick to her stomach just thinking about it.

She also knew in her heart that she didn't want him to move on. She *liked* him. Never mind that every time she saw him her heart skipped a beat and her thoughts wanted to turn to sex. Sex was no solution, not for either of them.

Although it might be quite a nice experience, she thought with a faint little smile as she mounted the porch steps. She certainly experienced a strong itch to run her hands all over that powerful body of Liam's.

He might have built it to fight demons, but wherever it had come from, it was a beaut.

She'd spent three days watching his muscles ripple in the sun and admiring them. They'd begun to invade her thoughts on waking and when she fell asleep. Heat pooled between her legs all too often, and she wondered if she was just lonely or in danger of developing a dangerous obsession with a man she hardly knew.

Oddly, the thoughts no longer made her feel guilty as they had at first. Good, because lately she'd become as determined to move on as Liam seemed to be determined to come to grips with himself and what he could still do.

Chet would have hated for her to keep moping. He had hated moping. How often had he said, "Life deals, and then you deal."

The memory brought another smile to her face. He'd been right. His other favorite saying was, "Life is what happens while you're making other plans." She'd heard that quote attributed to John Lennon as well as an early-twentieth-century writer. She supposed the source didn't matter as much as the sentiment. Besides, it was seldom that only one person had a particular idea.

All of which was a distraction. She set the lemonade on the small porch table and sat in one of the lawn chairs they'd always meant to replace with something sturdier. Well, maybe she'd get out the plans for those Adirondack chairs and see if she and Liam could work their way through them. Maybe it was time for her to get handy, too.

Ransom Laird was coming closer, she realized. She didn't see him out this way often. She had a lot of neighbors she often didn't see for weeks at a time or longer because running a ranch of any kind tended to be time-consuming. She'd have gotten to that point, too, once Chet had come home for good.

Except he wasn't going to do that now. And now she had Liam to concern her. Maybe she needed to look into getting some animals.

"Howdy," Ransom said as he rode up. He dismounted and tied his horse to the porch rail.

"Lemonade?" Sharon asked.

"I'd love some." He took a seat as she poured. Even in his early sixties, Ransom was the kind of man who could make a woman's heart flutter. Something about all that hard work outdoors, Sharon supposed.

"How's Mandy?" she asked.

"On a deadline," he said. "She may look up from her computer again in a couple of weeks. In the meantime, the boys and I are batching it. I throw her a sandwich from time to time."

Sharon laughed. "Isn't she successful enough to give herself more time?"

"She could have all the time she wants, but she says if she didn't set a tight deadline she'd probably never finish a book. I don't get it, but that's the way she operates. So you have a handyman?"

"Are people talking?"

"When do I get to talk to people? Now, if sheep could gossip, that might be something else. No, I saw him painting when I came up. Did I scare him off?"

"Maybe. I don't know. Liam was Chet's best buddy in the army and he came here to deliver a letter."

Ransom's face tightened. "So what's going on?"

"TBI."

He swore. "So you took him under your wing?"

"I'm not sure who is under whose wing, honestly. I needed some things done and he needed a place to stop."

"Nowhere to go?"

"Evidently not."

Ransom leaned back, sipping lemonade. "Mmm, that's good lemonade. Mandy did that for me, you know. Gave me a place to stop. It was supposed to be temporary, while I healed, but obviously that changed."

"I didn't know that." She had heard vague mentions that Ransom had been a CIA agent who had been tortured before coming here a couple of decades ago, but had had no idea Mandy had taken him in. Someday she wanted to get the full story.

"We don't talk about it a lot. Anyway, all I'm saying is, good for you. Sometimes a person just needs a place to slow down without stuff crashing in all the time. This is a good place for that. And if he's looking for some work after he's through with the painting, I might be able to use some help. If he's interested in sheep, anyway."

"Thanks, Ransom. I was thinking just a little while ago that maybe it's time I got some animals out here."

"Chet always planned to," he agreed. "Although I'm not sure all of *us* would have liked his choices."

She had to laugh. "I'm sure the wolves would have been impossible."

"Most likely. I'm hearing we have two packs up in the mountains now. No incidents yet, but some are getting edgy."

"Aw, no."

"Aw, yes. It's come up a few times at the grange meetings. There's a relatively simple solution, though."

"Which is?"

"Cowboys and good dogs, but I know some folks are running on the thinnest of margins. I'm thinking maybe we need to chip in and buy some really good herding dogs for those that are worried. We'll see. Money's tight, like, everywhere."

"Linc Blair, one of the teachers I work with, uses dogs. In fact, he gives a lot of his pups away, but I doubt he has enough of them to meet demand."

"I've talked to him. He's got some ideas." Ransom drained his lemonade and declined the offer of more. "Gotta get back to work. Sorry I didn't get to meet Liam. Say hi for me."

"I will."

"But the main reason I stopped by is that we're having a barbecue at our place the first Saturday of next month. I hope you can come, and bring Liam if he's willing."

"Thanks." Sharon smiled. "I love barbecues. What do I need to bring?"

"Now, that's something you'll have to call Mandy about. Don't expect her to answer the phone, though. She'll get back to you or have one of the boys call. But right now she's planning it as a celebration for finishing her book."

Rising, he touched the brim of his hat in farewell and descended the steps to his horse. Right then, Liam came around the corner of the house. He froze, his face tight.

Ransom went utterly still, reacting to Liam's evident hesitation. Sharon wondered what to do to bridge this awkward gap.

"Hi," Liam said finally, breaking the silence.

"Hello," Ransom answered. Holding his horse's reins, he took a step toward Liam and held out his hand.

"Ransom Laird. Those are my sheep that have been baa-ing at you."

Liam shook his hand. "Liam O'Connor. It's a soothing sound, actually. They don't seem to get upset about much."

"They're pretty placid most of the time," Ransom agreed. "Sorry to have to say hi and run, but work calls. You're welcome to the barbecue at my place in a few weeks. Sharon has the information." Again, he touched the brim of his hat with a finger and swung up into the saddle. "Pleasure to meet you, Liam."

He rode off at a slow gallop toward the distant herd of sheep.

Liam remained where he was, looking at Sharon. "Seems like a nice man."

"He always has been. The barbecue isn't for a few weeks yet, so you can think about it. Lemonade?"

"Thanks."

"Let me get a fresh glass." She carried Ransom's inside and returned quickly with a pair of glasses. She poured for both of them and then resumed her seat. At last, Liam came to sit on the other side of the table from her.

"I'm sorry," he said.

"For what?" She had seen his reaction earlier when he'd stood at the foot of the ladder, a man prepared for attack. "For being you?"

"For being rude."

"Hardly. He was still on the horizon when you walked away. You might not have seen him."

"But I did."

"And I told you who he was." She held the icy glass

of lemonade, watching condensation form on its side. "What happened exactly?"

"I realized that I'm not fit to cope with ordinary life. It makes me angry sometimes."

"You may not be fit right now, but you'll get there." She spoke firmly.

"You can't know that."

"I can't? You got used to being in combat. Surely you'll get used to a peaceful environment. TBI not-withstanding, you strike me as very adaptable, so don't write yourself off yet."

He didn't argue with her, but she didn't know if that was good or not. In so many ways, as revealing as he was about some things, he remained inscrutable. Either there was a lot he didn't want to discuss, or things he simply couldn't.

She sipped lemonade and stared out over the fields, which were beginning to simmer now as the afternoon warmed up. Emotional truths were the hardest to express. Sometimes all the words in the dictionary weren't enough.

"Painting," he said suddenly.

She looked at him. "What?"

"I was painting. I left the stuff sitting there. It'll kill the brush and roller if they dry out."

"The barn is killing the brushes," she said humor-ously. "And the rollers, come to think of it. All that rough wood. Don't worry."

"I finish what I start. Unless I forget."

Those last three words were so sardonic that her heart squeezed. "Clearly you didn't forget." She put her glass down. "Let's go take care of it. Like you, I need to be busy, too."

She saw his eyebrows rise.

"You think you're the only one who needs not to think about some things?"

He didn't answer, but there was no mistaking the flicker of pain that crossed his face. "Sometimes I forget…"

"That I'm Chet's widow? Sometimes, if I'm lucky, I forget, too." That sounded harsh, but it was true. She was stuck here, living a life, and forgetfulness could sometimes provide the only balm.

She jumped up and headed toward the side of the barn where he'd been painting. He followed right on her heels.

"I could do more today," he told her.

"Sure. If you insist. But it's getting kind of warm, and I'd rather not see you fall from that ladder. You haven't eaten in hours."

"I can handle the heat."

"I'm sure you can. But if you don't mind, I'd rather not chance it. There are other things that need doing if you need to keep busy."

The paint had only just started to skin over, so it was easy enough to plunge the brush and roller into a bucket for soaking, and to rinse out the pan. The tiny amount of paint in the can didn't seem worth the trouble, so she asked him to seal it up and put it on the stack of cans Ed would pick up for recycling.

She sent him to shower while she made sandwiches for lunch. When he returned, he was wearing fresh but paint-spattered clothes. Well, of course. He'd arrived with only a backpack. He probably had only a few changes.

She didn't have anything around that might fit him, and didn't know if he could handle shopping.

Putting her chin in her hand, she watched him eat and thought about how complicated all of this was. She wondered if it really had to be this complicated. Dancing around everything only made it harder for both of them. He'd been blunt when he arrived. Maybe it was time for her to be blunt, too.

"I need to go to town." She wasn't exactly prepared for feeding two, and she needed to remedy that. But there was another need now, too. "How about you get yourself some more clothes?"

He looked down at himself.

"You hardly want to go everywhere covered with primer and barn-red. And you might want some cooler clothes. Summer's really arriving."

He thought about it, saying little while he ate another few bites. Then he startled her. "More clothes imply a commitment."

Astonished, her mouth hung open. "A commitment? How?"

"More to keep me here."

She didn't know whether to get mad or not. Seriously, that was either crazy or opaque. "Do you have a problem with being here for a while? Or is it inconceivable that you could just leave your messed-up clothes behind whenever you want to go?"

Now he looked a little surprised. "I must have said that wrong."

"Maybe so." She was glad when the phone rang. Jumping up, she went to answer it. It turned out to be the mother of one of her students from the past year who wanted to know if she might consider tutoring her younger son in math.

"I don't know if he's just unwilling or if he's just not getting it, but you did such a good job with Mike, I thought you might be able to help Andy."

"I'd be glad to tutor if you don't mind bringing Andy over here." No way was she going to drive all over the county. She'd learned that two summers ago, when she started tutoring one girl and wound up with half a dozen students who were scattered around the county as if someone had thrown a handful of jacks. She didn't know why, but once you took on one student, you acquired others. Last summer, she had been too raw to even consider it, but this year it would be welcome.

After she hung up she found that Liam had finished his lunch and was carrying his plate to the dishwasher. "So you work over the summer, too?" he asked.

"Just a little. Some tutoring. I like it. One-on-one interaction is very satisfying."

"Like teaching me to read."

"Yes. I get something out of it, too, Liam."

Those light green eyes of his creased at the corners with something like a smile. "Glad to hear it."

"I wouldn't be a teacher otherwise."

He closed the dishwasher door. "What were we talking about before?"

She waited, giving him the opportunity to recall if he could.

His expression brightened another shade. "Town. Clothes."

"Yes." She bit back the urge to question him again about what he meant by commitment. The possibilities in those words might be painful. She wasn't ready to admit that she liked having him around, because that would mean it would be painful when he left. And he would leave. There was no reason on Earth for him to hang around here once he felt he had his feet under him. And day by day she watched him growing a little more confident. The work must be helping.

Maybe that was most of what he needed, a sense that he could be useful again. She definitely understood that need.

She knew he was going through a difficult time, but she hadn't expected it to be so difficult for her, as well. The Liam she had heard about was a competent soldier and a great friend. The man she had met was still powerful, but facing difficulties, some physical, some emotional. She couldn't examine all this thoroughly and didn't intend to. The important thing to her was that he kept trying. As each new thing came up, whether going to town, eating in a restaurant, painting or learning to read, he insisted on trying it.

But it was painful, nonetheless, to have some idea of what he had once been, and to see him struggle now to get himself back.

"Clothes," he said again. "I need clothes."

It was like watching a man remember where he was, even though he'd only briefly wandered away.

He looked at her. "Okay. What clothes do I need?"

She hesitated. "How about you decide that? I have a washer, so it's not like you need a whole lot. Go for comfort."

He looked down at himself and said with humor, "Just stuff that isn't covered in paint." Then he asked her, "What are you going to be doing in town?"

"Buying groceries. The larder is getting low, to put it mildly."

"You should let me help pay for them."

"Good heavens, why? You're working your butt off to help me out."

"The question," he said with amazing insight, "is who is helping who."

She managed not to correct his grammar. The thought was good enough. "Maybe a little of both, big guy. Let me grab my purse, and we'll go."

It actually felt good to be heading into town again. During the school year, she made enough trips on weekdays that she tried to avoid them on weekends. Last summer, she had practically holed up, though, and this summer had been headed the same direction prior to Liam's arrival. She supposed she had a lot to be grateful to him for. He was slowly digging her out of her shell.

Of course, emerging from a shell meant becoming vulnerable again, open to the bad that life brought as well as the good. Still, she enjoyed the fresh air blowing through her rolled-down window, the view of the mountains and the fields they passed, the sense of being out of her rut even if it was just to visit the grocery.

Before heading on to the grocery, she pulled into a parking place in front of Freitag's Mercantile. "This is it," she said. "The only place in town to buy some clothes."

Liam didn't climb out immediately, simply watched the street, the handful of people coming and going, as if he were getting his bearings. She almost offered to come in with him, then reminded herself this was a man who had navigated his way halfway across the country to bring her a letter. She waited patiently, allowing him whatever space he might need.

Then he smiled at her. "I'll be out front when you're done."

"Good enough."

She watched him climb out and walk into the store, the only hesitation that faint hitch in his stride. God, he was a hunk. Simply watching him walk away was enough to get her all hot and bothered. She squirmed a little in her seat and fought to redirect her thoughts to a safer place.

It struck her then that she might have seriously underestimated him. This was not a man who feared anything, except possibly the glitches inside his own head.

He was more than ready to wrap his hands around life and deal with it. The TBI might have left him with some deficits, and made him uncertain about what he could do, but apart from anxiety and anger, both of which she had read were normal for TBI survivors, he most definitely wasn't afraid to plunge in.

If he feared anything at all, it was his own reactions.

As she backed out and drove on to the market, she reviewed her own reactions and assessments.

It struck her that she'd been guilty of diminishing him, too. For all she kept giving him chances to do things, part of her didn't expect him to succeed. How had she fallen into that trap?

Because, answered the utterly truthful part of her mind, it made her safe from the sexual attraction she'd been trying to bury since day one. And man, what an attraction, like a match she just couldn't blow out. So she was trying to evade those feelings by concentrating on his lacks.

Like just now, she could have offered to shop with him. She could have helped him pick out clothes. The impulse was there, but it was a mothering impulse, not the way you treated another adult. She kept having those urges and needed to stop them. Especially since they were purely defensive ones, and unfair to him.

Working her way through the store, filling a cart with things she had already learned that Liam seemed to like, and plenty of fresh greens for herself, she found herself remembering how he looked standing on that ladder just yesterday when the afternoon's temperature had started rising and he'd shed his shirt.

Muscles, shiny with sweat, rippling with every movement. No wonder she wanted to put a safe barrier between them.

Well, it might protect her, but it wouldn't do him a darn bit of good. He needed to find his own way through this. All she could provide were some opportunities to explore, like reading and painting. Maybe some other work around the place.

But the bottom line was, he wasn't her charge, he wasn't her student and he was a man in every sense of the word.

Coming out of the grocery with what she hoped would be enough to keep them fed for a week—his appetite was growing the longer he painted—she felt a sense of relief, as if she had let go of something that had been weighing her down.

She knew exactly what it was: she no longer had to see him as anything but the attractive man he was. And now she could give in to the sexual twinges he aroused in her without the sense of taking advantage.

She almost laughed at herself as she loaded groceries into the back of the truck. He hadn't done one damn thing to make her feel like he felt the same attraction for her. Not one.

So it was a safe little fantasy, and she could stop throwing up mental roadblocks and just enjoy feeling like a woman again, instead of asexual. That was a trick she had learned while Chet was away. It sometimes amazed her how often men seemed to think a woman couldn't get by for months on end while her husband was away. A few had even made passes at her a few months after the funeral.

So yeah, she'd learned to put that feminine, sexual part of herself on ice. Except now there was no reason not to thaw it out a bit. She had needs, too. Dreaming about them couldn't be a crime.

Liam stood on the sidewalk in front of Freitag's, watching the area. There were few people about as it was a weekday, but those few that passed him did so with a smile and nod. He was still getting used to not having to be on high alert in situations like this, but the adjustment was getting steadily more comfortable.

He held two bags containing a few shirts, shorts and jeans, as well as some changes of underwear. It hadn't been a big trip, nor a taxing one. He wasn't especially worried about clothes, and choosing had been simple because he didn't care as long as it fit. The clerk had been nice, troubling him very little as he selected things.

In short, he was feeling pretty good. Other than stops on the road to grab something to eat from convenience stores, this was his first real shopping trip, and he'd managed it. Maybe Sharon was right. Maybe he could do more than he thought, and just needed a chance to find out.

He was even feeling pretty pleased with having figured out a method to simplify the decision-making.

He almost felt like grinning.

In less than a week since he'd been here, he was already feeling a whole lot better than when he'd arrived. He had work he was enjoying, he felt useful again, he was making some progress with reading, however slowly, and he was reentering the world in minor ways.

He'd even just applied one mental list to a different task: dressing to shopping.

Sharon pulled up in front, and he tossed his bags into the back and climbed in the cab with her.

"How'd it go?" she asked as she pulled away.

"Just fine." He looked at her and answered her smile with one of his own. "Just fine," he repeated.

"Great." Her smile widened. "What did you get?"

For a moment he drew a blank, but then it came back. "Clothes." Then it struck him that answer was too abbreviated. "Do you really want to know all about it?"

She glanced at him, arching a brow. "Of course I do."

"I suppose for most people it would be pretty boring."

"Not to me," she said quietly. "Seems like you took a pretty big step."

He felt surprisingly touched by how aware she was, and how encouraging. He'd been on the road long enough to have run into folks who had names for him, many of them unflattering.

"Well, I remembered what I went in there for. That doesn't sound like a big deal but—"

She interrupted. "That's a real big deal. I remember

you telling me how much difficulty you have following through on a task."

"Yeah. So I remembered that. When I told the lady I wanted clothes and could she show me where, she walked me over. Nice of her. I'm still not sure I can remember directions unless I write them down."

"We'll work on that and find out," she said firmly. "Maybe we'll even practice."

"It might work," he said. "Then I picked out clothes. But you know what was cool, Sharon?"

"Yes?"

"I remembered what I needed by walking myself mentally through getting dressed in the morning. I laid the stuff out on the sale table in that order so I wouldn't forget anything."

"That was brilliant," she said warmly.

"You don't have to patronize me," he said, then caught himself. "Sorry. I get touchy sometimes."

"It's okay. We all get touchy. But I meant that sincerely. Look, you memorized a series of actions and then you used them to do something else. There are plenty of people who can't make that leap. I ought to know. I teach."

He saw she was smiling out the windshield and it made him feel good. "It was great to realize I'd done that. Now I'm wondering what else I can get to that way."

"And what else you may know how to do that you just don't know yet. I mean, did I have to tell you how to paint? Any part of it? Heck, no."

That was true, he thought. He might not know what half the tools in the barn were for, at least not yet, and he might get overwhelmed by some things, but he had known how to get out a ladder and how to paint. He had even remembered how to clean the brushes and rollers.

They had said he would probably continue to improve, but today he was feeling more hopeful of that than anytime since he'd walked out the door of rehab.

"Thank you," he said.

"For what? I should be thanking you."

He shook his head. "I've been out of rehab for a few weeks now. Wandering around, using a map on which I'd marked out my route, but with nothing else to do. No future, no plans beyond getting Chet's letter to you. I had to stick to eating from convenience stores where I could see the food because I couldn't read. Well, you saw that at the diner. Menus are beyond me right now. Too many things crammed together, and sometimes funky type."

She nodded, but remained silent, listening. He was glad she didn't try to respond.

"Sometimes," he said, "I even forgot why I was on the road. So I had it written on the map—get to Chet's wife. The only thing I didn't ever forget was Chet's letter."

A soft, sad sound escaped her, but she still didn't interrupt.

"Sometimes I'd get so frustrated I exploded. At least I didn't get into any trouble. They got that part through to me in rehab. Walk away, explode in private. But damn, when I couldn't read a sign, or figure out how much something cost, or what it really was inside a package, sometimes I'd just want to blow. Some people noticed I wasn't that bright, too."

She sucked a breath. "Did they say things?"

"Of course. I guess they thought I was too stupid or too mental to understand. Or maybe they didn't care."

"Did you get angry?"

"At them?" He shrugged. "Hell, if anyone knows I got problems, it's me. Sometimes I said things back, though. I told you, I think, that sometimes I just say whatever comes to mind."

"I haven't seen too much of that."

"Being around you is easy. Things are simple, undemanding. I don't know if you're being careful of me or what, but you make it uncomplicated. And sometimes I still don't know if I'm making sense. Things come out and then I'm not sure what I said. Were the words right? Did I say it wrong? If you ever wonder, just ask, okay? I'd like that better than you thinking I said something I didn't mean."

"Okay." Then, "I'm sorry people said things. Sometimes we're so heartless."

"It's just people. I'll probably say a lot of things I shouldn't before I'm done. Probably more than most. I remember one guy, though. I was picking up a couple of sandwiches at this gas station, and I was talking myself through it. Maybe more than usual because I was getting tired. I got two turkey sandwiches."

Then he fell silent. What had he been saying? The last words he heard in his mind were "turkey sandwiches." Where had he been going before that? "Damn!"

"Liam?"

"I forgot what I was saying." Damn, a moment ago he'd been feeling so good and now the frustration was eating into him like acid. He tried to recover the feelings before his brain had slipped a stupid cog, but the frustration was too much.

"You know," he said in a burst, "if I had to be left with strong feelings, it would have been nice if they'd been good ones!"

"What exactly are you feeling?"

"Frustration. I want to smash something."

"Because you can't remember what you were saying or because of something else?"

The question drew him up short, his frustration easing just a bit. "I don't know," he said finally. "Is it the glitch in my head or is it really that I forgot what I was saying? How the hell am I supposed to know the difference?"

"I don't know."

He pounded his fist on his knee, then caught himself. "Sorry," he said dully. "I'm not supposed to do that."

He turned his head, looking out at the passing countryside without seeing it. He could no longer remember why he'd gotten so frustrated. He just was. More words burst out of him, directed at the window.

"It's like being in a bag I can't even see. I don't know how the hell to get out, or even where it is."

All of sudden, a small, warm hand covered the fist that still rested on his knee. She didn't say anything. He wasn't sure he would even have heard her if she had. But the touch helped. In some amazing way, it helped.

He didn't say another word until they got home.

Chapter Six

Over the next week, Liam worked like a demon. Sharon was beginning to get concerned because he wouldn't slow down. Maybe he was working on some private exorcism, but that barn was getting covered with primer faster than she would have believed possible for one man. He started right after breakfast, took ten minutes to eat some lunch outside, then was back at it until the light started to fail.

She started tutoring Andy in math, but that only took a small amount of time. Once again, days stretched before her endlessly as they had before Liam's arrival. Except that she had his company after dinner, which was pleasant enough.

But something had changed, and she wished she knew what. She canceled the weekend card game with her friends, feeling that might be uncomfortable for him, so she didn't even have that to look forward to.

Not good, she thought as she stood on her back porch and watched Liam painting the last of the barn. Not good. Before his arrival, she'd been wrestling with the fact that she needed to make some changes, then he'd shown up and everything had changed. She had a purpose again.

Now she was back to square one. Her own fault, she supposed, for filling the emptiness with trying to help one man. She needed to be looking further afield and further down the road than that. Her life had changed irrevocably with the loss of Chet, and like it or not, she had some serious rebuilding to do. Apparently, Liam was just another postponement.

Except she didn't want to think that way, or look at him that way. That created an internal conflict for her because it was making her view herself in an uncomfortable light.

Had she pinned too much on one man? Had she somehow lost all her internal resources with Chet? Could she get them back?

Even knowing all Liam's problems, or at least the most significant ones, she didn't see him as diminished in any way. He was a good man, a kind man, struggling with problems she could understand technically, but never really know from the inside.

And watching him work out there in the afternoon sun reminded her that he was very much a man. The attraction she felt kept growing, and nothing that happened diminished it in the least.

But for some reason, he seemed to have pulled back within a shell. Working constantly, spending time on the reading lessons, polite in every way, but withdrawn. He had definitely pulled away for some reason, and inevitably she wondered what she might have done wrong.

She couldn't think of anything. One minute he'd been happy about a successful shopping trip, and then the frustration had settled in like a dark storm and he'd gone away to some place within himself. It was almost as if he'd packed up and left.

Why?

As she watched those gleaming muscles ripple even at this distance, she felt undeniable twinges of longing and desire. He was a magnificent man. What's more, out here with physical labor, his problems largely vanished.

But she had to be careful, she realized. Careful that she wasn't suffering from some kind of rescue complex, that she really saw him as a capable adult, an equal.

Maybe that was why he'd thrown himself into that painting in this almost manic way. Maybe he was proving that to himself, too.

She sighed and started to turn to go inside and make lunch.

"Sharon?"

At the sound of Liam's call, she turned back. He was dismounting the ladder, holding the pan and brushes.

Automatically she started walking toward him, reminding herself to remain as casual as possible despite the storm of conflict within her. She had to deal with her own feelings, not inflict them on him.

While she crossed the yard, he ascended the ladder again and brought down the rest of his supplies. She arrived just as he reached the ground once more.

He surprised her with his first smile in days. "I'll be done with the primer today."

"You're doing a wonderful job," she said warmly. "But, Liam, aren't you working too hard?"

His gaze shifted from her to the distance, although it gave her the feeling that he was staring into himself, not at the neighboring mountains.

"I need it," he said finally.

She wasn't going to argue that. "I just don't want you to get heatstroke or something."

"This isn't hot."

She wondered if he was comparing it to Iraq, where he and Chet had both served for a time, but for around here this was warm, indeed. She remained silent.

"Thank you," he said finally, "for your concern. I know my limits."

Well, at least that was a positive statement. The first really confident one he'd given her. "Did you want to show me something?"

His gaze came back to her. "Show you something?"

"You called me," she reminded him.

"Oh." His brow creased. Then it smoothed just a bit. "Apologize," he said.

"Me? For what?" Her heart skipped as she wondered what she had done.

"Not you. Me." He sighed and ran his fingers through hair that had grown noticeably since his arrival. "I was going to apologize."

"No need. All you've done is a fantastic painting job."

"Not that." He closed his eyes a few seconds and she could almost feel his internal struggle to grip some thought. "I've been ignoring you."

She started to say that he'd been working awfully

hard but decided to just remain quiet and let him follow his thought train.

"It's not right," he said in a burst, "to want your best friend's wife."

Shock held her frozen. Blunt? Incredibly. But honest. And hadn't she struggled with the same thing? She should speak. Or maybe not. God, she didn't know the right thing to do, so she waited for whatever else he might say, her heart sinking then rising like a bouncing ball, up and down. Desire drizzled through her at his blunt declaration, awakening all the things she'd been trying to keep sleeping.

"You should send me on my way. As soon as I finish painting."

At that, she could no longer remain silent. "Why? And to what?"

"What do you mean what?"

"What do you do next, Liam? What's the plan when you walk away from here?"

"Damn it, I don't want to be an adopted stray!"

The words exploded out of him, the fury unmistakable. The dimensions of his problem were becoming clear. But she had a bit of a temper, too, and while it might have been the wrong way to respond, she erupted right back.

"I'm not rescuing a stray! You've been helping me. What I want from you is a plan!"

"I can't make plans." He glared at her.

"So I gather. But you were Chet's best friend. Do you think he'd let you walk away from here without a plan? A job? A place to go? Would you let him if he were in your shoes?" It occurred to her that question might be beyond him still, but she was relieved to find it wasn't.

"Of course not."

"Then shut up. You're doing an incredible amount of stuff for me that wouldn't be getting done except for you. I owe you big-time. I think about it constantly."

It was his turn to remain silent, simply looking at her.

"And let's get one other thing clear," she said, still feeling hot in more ways than one. "I'm not Chet's wife anymore. I'm his widow. That's a whole different thing. I got used to it, now *you* get used to it."

Turning, she nearly ran toward the house. Tears burned in her eyes, though whether from sorrow or anger she didn't know. Sorrow for Chet, certainly, but sorrow for Liam now, too. And anger because she was doing an incredibly poor job of getting her feelings across to him.

To occupy herself and work out her own frustration, she made a tuna salad and started piling it onto rye bread. The man must be starved, and maybe she'd calm down enough to eat something herself.

Just as she was placing the plates on the table, the back door opened, and he stepped in. His clothes were paint covered, and she cleared the way to the sink so he could wash his hands.

"I'm sorry," he said.

"Quit apologizing. There's not one damn thing you need to apologize for."

"Okay."

She sat at the table, out of the way, waiting for him to scrub his hands and forearms. At last he joined her, facing her across the tile and two lunch plates, his brimming with three sandwiches and some chips.

He didn't say anything as he started to eat. Of course not. He wasn't much of a conversation starter. When he did speak first, it often seemed to come out of nowhere. She was getting used to that, but she often wondered what roads his thoughts wandered down.

"You're opaque sometimes," she said finally.

That got his attention. He stopped chewing, swallowed and looked up from his plate. "Opaque?"

"Yeah. For a guy who told me he often says things he shouldn't, and says too much, you turn into a sphinx a lot."

"Sphinx?" It took a moment, but he made the connection. "That's good."

"It is? Why?"

"Because they spent a lot of time teaching me not to say the first thing that popped into my head."

She thought of what he'd said out at the barn, then decided not to mention the obvious: he didn't always succeed. Surprisingly, she was glad of that.

"Just talk," she said finally. "It'd be nice to know where we both stand. We might fight sometimes, but the air will be a whole lot clearer. I'm spending entirely too much time wondering what you're thinking, if I've said or done something wrong."

"That's not good."

"No, it's not. Hey, are you afraid of a squabble?"

He astonished her then by laughing. "No," he admitted.

"So talk. Squabbles are useful, too."

"Okay. I remember there was something I was going to tell you when we were coming home from town, but I can't remember what. Losing my train of thought frustrates me. It makes me mad. So I started painting to work it out in a safe way."

"You've been painting like a demon."

"Maybe not smart. Working keeps the frustration down, but it lets my head wander too much. And then I get aware that I get lost sometimes in what I'm thinking, just the way I get lost when I'm talking."

"And that makes you madder."

He stared at the sandwich he held. "I can remember not being this way. Sometimes I think it would be better if I couldn't remember at all."

That was so unutterably sad that she felt her eyes burn again. "Liam?" Her voice sounded choked.

"What?"

"I'm glad you can remember even if it's hard. Even if it hurts. Even if it frustrates you. Without a memory… you wouldn't be you anymore. And I like you."

His head snapped up, his odd light green eyes fixing on her. "I'm not very likable."

"Says who?"

"Plenty of people."

"Tell me one." It wasn't a challenge; in fact, she kept her voice calm and even gentle.

"I don't need to tell you one. I can tell you lots. The ones who called me mental and stupid."

She bit her lip, and now the burning in her eyes transformed into an ache in her heart. "Those people don't know you and they don't know what they're talking about."

"They know what they see. That's how I look."

"Not to me. Not even the first time we met." Her throat now hurt as if a noose was wrapped around it. Oh, God, she didn't want to break down and cry. He might misread it.

"I like painting. I'm not stupid when I do that."

She swallowed the pain she felt for him. "No, you're not. In fact, you're pretty damn good."

"I remembered how."

"Exactly. No help from anyone."

He nodded slowly. "But what's next again?"

"The barn needs paint over the primer."

"Right." He repeated the words. "As soon as I finish."

"Ed will deliver the paint tomorrow."

"Good. Then what?"

"Should we make a list?" At least he wasn't talking about hitting the road again, although she suspected that might come back.

He met her gaze again. "I'd like to try to remember. If I forget again, then we can make a list."

Her chest swelled as she realized he was back to making an effort, that he'd stopped trying to hide his frustration, stopped trying to hide from her, stopped trying to think leaving was the only answer. "Sounds good to me."

He resumed eating and she didn't press him again. Her own stomach had loosened up enough that she felt able to take a bite of her sandwich.

Then he surprised her. "Let's make a list," he said. "A long list of all the things you want done. After the barn. The longer the better."

"Sure." She didn't question him. Maybe the list would give him a sense that he had a direction and a plan beyond tomorrow. It sounded like a good idea, actually. Maybe she ought to make one for herself, too. Things that she could do that she should have been doing. Giving up on the ranch because her dream with Chet had vanished might not have been wise.

No, maybe not. Maybe she should have gone ahead

with as much of the dream as she could manage on her own, because it had been her dream, too, not just Chet's.

She spoke. "Should you give up a dream of your own just because the person you shared it with is gone?"

"No." The answer came surprisingly fast.

She lifted her eyes to him. "What are your dreams, Liam?"

"Feeling normal again, even if I'm not."

"That's a good one. I think you'll get at least that far, if not well beyond it."

"I hope so. What dream are you talking about?"

"Having some livestock here. Maybe I can't do the whole rescue thing, but I could get a couple of goats."

"Why couldn't you do the rescue thing?"

She smiled wryly. "Because the way Chet had it planned out, it was going to be a full-time job for at least one of us. I still have to teach this fall."

He nodded. "That was going to be his retirement."

"Pretty much."

"But it wasn't just his dream."

"Not at all. I wanted it, too. He just kept making it bigger and bigger."

Liam chuckled. "For a fact. I listened to it. So start small. I can help at least for now. I think Chet always intended to drag me into this."

A little bubble of laughter escaped her. "I think you're right. I lost count of the times we'd be talking about those plans and out would come, 'Liam and I will...' How did you feel about that?"

"Truthfully? It was nice that he wanted me to be part of it, but I wasn't really sure it was my thing. How would I know? I was a city kid."

"But he dragged you into helping in Afghanistan."

"He sure did. I liked it, too."

"So maybe I'll put that on my personal to-do list. Get a few goats to start. I'll see how it goes."

"And if you don't like it?"

"I have a neighbor," she said dryly. "He probably wouldn't mind a few extra goats, especially since I'll likely buy these from him."

He smiled, and she realized that whatever had been bugging him seemed to have passed.

Good, she thought as he returned to finish the barn. It would probably only take him an hour or so at this point. But she couldn't stop remembering his words, *it's not right to want your best friend's wife.*

They drummed in her head and seemed to pulse between her legs. She shouldn't want her husband's best friend, either.

But the situation had changed. Afghanistan had changed it irrevocably.

"We didn't have kids," she announced over dinner to Liam. Why, she didn't know. Maybe because she was thinking about giving Ransom a call and he had children. Everyone, just about, had children.

"Why not?" he asked. He seemed to like the roast chicken and green bean casserole as much as Chet had.

"Because… You know, sometimes I wonder if I was selfish."

His expression grew perplexed. "Why?"

"Because I didn't want to have any children as long as Chet was going into combat. I didn't want to raise a child alone."

"Did that bother him?"

Apparently, this was something Chet had never discussed with his best friend. In some way it relieved her to know that some things had remained between the two of them, unlike paint chips and fabric samples. "He said he understood."

Liam pondered that. "Chet didn't lie."

"No, he didn't. So we waited." She stared into space, remembering. It had seemed to make so much sense at the time, but now she wondered. What if she'd had a small version of Chet running around for the past year and a half? Would it have helped? Would she have had something more important to focus on than herself?

And then there was the fact that now there was nothing of Chet left but this ranch. Would he have been content with that legacy?

"Do you feel bad about it now?"

The question called her back. "I'm not sure. It seems wrong somehow that he didn't leave a son."

"It might have been a girl," he said bluntly. "And either way, the kid would never have really known him. So what are you talking about here? Genes?"

God, he *could* be blunt. He'd warned her, after all.

"Well, that sounds stupid," she said irritably.

"Just reducing it to the bottom line. The gene thing? A lot of people get hung up on that. I get it. But considering that I read somewhere that we're all more closely related than we'd believe, it also gets a little silly. Last name carried on? Well, maybe you'll find a guy who'd be willing to let a child carry Chet's last name."

She gaped at him. This conversation was going sideways fast, heading to places she never would have imagined. "Yeah, right," she said finally.

"I would," he said with a shrug. "What's a name? How many people named Majors are there in the world? Thousands probably. The world is overrun with O'Connors."

"You," she said, "are something else."

"Why? Because I don't get hung up on this whole thing? I guess. A lot of people think it's important. I just never figured it that way. I read somewhere that you can't take a genealogy back more than four hundred years because everybody starts being related to you. Two thousand years and everybody on the planet is related. So Chet's genes are out there in lots of places. After all, he got them from somewhere. That leaves a name."

"That also leaves," she said tautly, "an emotional connection."

His expression dimmed. "I just put my foot in it again, didn't I?"

At once she felt that squeezing ache that was becoming all too familiar with him. She didn't want him to feel bad, and she knew she wasn't being entirely rational. This thought had reared up to plague her more than once since Chet's passing, and why the hell it had come up tonight she wasn't sure. Except that she was thinking about getting goats, and getting goats from Ransom probably meant he'd show up with his son to help and…and what?

"I'm sorry you regret it," he said. "I was stupid to talk that way."

"You're not stupid," she said, expressing her pain with a little anger. "Stop saying that!"

"I made you mad. Maybe hurt you."

"You didn't hurt me." She wanted to put her head in her hands and find a way through this morass she had just created. Instead, she sought a plateau within herself, the place where she could remain calm even when she had twenty kids in a classroom erupting simultaneously. "You were being logical."

"And you reminded me that logic isn't always right."

"It's different, is all." Bit by bit she was finding her equilibrium. "You're right. I made a decision. Chet agreed with it. It's ridiculous at this point to regret it. It is what it is. And logically you're right about what it means. But emotionally I sometimes wish I still had that connection with Chet. It's an emotional tug I can't explain very well. It's just there sometimes. But when I'm not feeling it the way I am tonight, I can see that maybe we weren't wrong to choose to wait. I'd have a little child now who would be fatherless. I'd have more to deal with and I haven't exactly been managing the best. Maybe it would have helped me to cope, but would that have been fair to a child?"

He answered slowly, but she couldn't tell if he was choosing his words with care or simply finding it difficult to follow that spate of nearly contradictory feelings.

"I don't know," he said finally.

"Neither do I, really. But sometimes I understand why people freeze eggs and sperm. Other times…" She shook her head. "Other times it's not an issue. It just bubbles up every now and then."

He nodded but didn't respond.

She sat there for a while, nibbling on her chicken, giving him space to eat, thinking about her reaction as opposed to his. Very different responses to what was, for her, a purely emotional question. She was still wondering why she had brought it up. Except…except… A thought struck her and she spoke it before she thought it through.

"Maybe I feel like a failure for not doing that one thing for Chet."

He stopped eating, his green eyes fixing on her. "Not doing...oh." He found his way back to the earlier conversation. "Chet didn't feel like you failed him in any way. I'm pretty damn sure of that. We spent a lot of years together in some tough places. We talked. He never had a complaint about you. Not even a little one."

That lightened her heart more than a little bit.

"I'm sorry," he volunteered, "that you didn't have more time together."

She drew a deep breath, not quite a sigh. "I've been getting used to it, Liam. Getting used to the fact that life doesn't make any promises to anyone. We all take the same chances. That was maybe the hardest part at first, feeling it wasn't fair. Life just isn't fair."

"No, it's not."

He probably knew that as well as anyone. She resisted reaching out to him across the table. "Well," she said brightly, "time to think about goats."

His brow lifted. "Seriously?"

"Seriously."

One corner of his mouth crooked upward. "Chet had me working with goats in Afghanistan a few times."

"Then you can help me."

For an instant, something like distress passed over his face. "I can remember," he reminded her, "but maybe not in a way that's useful."

"You remembered how to paint. Anyway, we'll learn together."

"I guess you're determined."

"I need to reclaim some part of myself." She needed to get on with her life. She'd been thinking that right before Liam arrived and for some reason, it seemed more important now. Something inside her was trying to break free and breathe again. Maybe this was the wrong way to go about it, but she needed to start somewhere.

"I guess I'll look at that pen out near the barn and make sure it'll hold up," she announced. "I need to know that before I do anything else."

"Okay. I'll try to help."

After they washed up the dishes, they went out into the long evening to take a look at the pen. As they approached the barn, Sharon noticed the smell of the fresh primer and commented on it. "That's a good smell after all this time. Usually when I come out this way, all I smell is musty wood."

"It smells pretty musty inside, too. Maybe I should clean it out."

"One thing at a time." She was feeling cheerful all of a sudden. The idea of having some goats to look after and enjoy really appealed to her. She ought to get a dog, too, now that she thought about it. Time to reconnect with life.

The evening had reached that wonderful point when the air had calmed, the light had dimmed and taken away the harshness, and the temperature had started to fall.

"It's beautiful tonight," she said in a burst of exuberance.

"Yes."

She looked at him and caught him smiling at her. The expression, so unguarded, was contagious and she grinned back. "I'm glad," she admitted, "to be alive."

His smile faded a bit and she could only imagine

what he must be thinking or remembering. Maybe she had been thoughtless in her remark?

But then he surprised her. "So am I." He sounded as if he meant it.

Well, good. "Anyway, it's about time I started looking forward again. There's too many years left to waste."

"Or maybe there's no years at all."

His words caught her between one breath and the next and she missed a step. God, he was so blunt sometimes, but he was also right. Nobody was guaranteed to be around tomorrow. And that trite truism struck her as incredibly profound all of a sudden.

"Live in the moment?" she asked.

"I seem to remember learning how to do that a long time ago. And lately that's pretty much all I seem to be able to do."

"Maybe that's smart in the long run."

He shrugged. "I don't know. Sometimes it's necessary."

"True. But I think I've been missing too many moments by living in the past and fearing the future."

"I can understand that."

She supposed he could. They reached the pen that Chet had put up during his last leave: metal poles and chain link. "Chet built this," she said. "He said it was for animals to be determined later. I think goats would be nice."

"Why goats?"

She looked at him. "Because I like them. They're smart, cute and much more impish than sheep."

"You want impish?"

"It'll be entertaining. What do you remember about the goats you'd worked with?"

"That you had to be a damn good goatherd with a damn good dog or two. They seemed to have a lot of curiosity in them."

"That was my impression. I suppose I could ask Ransom, though."

"He raises them, too?"

"Mostly it's sheep but he has some goats that he claims are more like pets. Maybe that's what I've been thinking about, the way he talks about them."

"Good to go to the expert." He looked out over the large penned area. "There's a lot of bushy stuff in there."

"Is that bad?"

"Not for goats."

She almost laughed. Evidently, he remembered something about the care and feeding of them. "Well, the pen looks like it's held up, anyway. I don't need to do anything immediately."

She started to walk around the large enclosure. "I guess I have a lot to learn before I go ahead with this." She pushed on posts to make sure they were still firmly planted, and scanned the chain link for any breaks.

He didn't say anything as he walked with her but she found some comfort in his silent company. She'd been alone for so damn long, she realized. Even her time with Chet had been rare, and while she'd filled her days with other things, the loneliness had remained.

"Did you know you can feel lonely even when you're busy and have a lot of friends simply because someone you love is gone?"

"I don't have much experience. Never had time for anything that wasn't casual."

"Well, you can. I spent a lot of time being lonely

when I was married. I accepted it, but I never got used to it."

"I'm sorry. Chet missed you all the time, too."

"He told me. I sometimes wonder about it."

"Why?"

"Because we actually spent so little time together overall. His absence was far more usual than his presence. You'd think you'd get used to it just because it was normal. Maybe it's just me."

He didn't answer, but what could he say? And why was she wandering this particular path? "I guess I'm still sorting things out."

"I think we spend our lives doing that."

"True." She wasn't watching her feet closely enough, and she stepped into a hole. A cry of surprise escaped her as she started to tumble forward.

Then powerful arms seized her, keeping her upright, and the next thing she knew, she leaned against a rock-hard chest.

"Are you okay?" he asked.

No, she wasn't okay. Everything she'd been trying not to notice about him, everything she'd been trying not to feel, came rushing in a dizzying wave to her consciousness. She wanted him. Hell, maybe she needed him. Maybe any man would have done after all this time, but she wasn't going to deal with that now.

Now, right now, being pressed against a man's hard, warm chest, wrapped in strong arms, surrounded by his scents, was an aphrodisiac beyond compare. Her body reacted and her mind shut down as every cell within her reminded her that she was a woman and she had needs.

Her nose pressed into him and she had the strongest

urge to just burrow in. Instead, she tilted her head back and looked up at him.

He looked straight at her, and everything in his gaze reflected the longing she was feeling. She held perfectly still, afraid of shattering the welder's arc of desire that was burning in her as it had not burned in so long.

How could she have forgotten this yearning, an ache so deep and so hard, it hurt? How could she have forgotten the magic of hanging suspended in an instant out of time, breathless with anticipation, on a knife edge of hope? How could she have forgotten how easy it could be to beg?

But before the words *oh, please* could escape her on a whisper of breath, his head lowered and his lips met hers.

Warm, firm lips, tentative as if he expected rejection. She wanted no part of that, not now. Sliding her hands up his arms, she gripped his shoulders, needing him even closer. She didn't want light, feathery touches, or seduction. She wanted hard and fast and basic before something, anything, intervened. Before a sensible thought had a chance to pop up.

Here, now, on the ground in the gloaming...just *now*.

Whatever he thought he'd forgotten, he hadn't forgotten how to interpret a woman's moves. The pressure of her grip on his shoulders caused him to kiss her harder, his tongue sliding over the crease of her lips demanding entry. She was only too happy to provide it.

The world washed away in a rising tide of physical sensations that seemed to clamp her in a vise. The hunger was almost painful, and each movement of his tongue stroking hers caused a spasm between her legs. Had she ever risen so far so fast?

Did it matter? She knew she was racing toward a pinnacle from little more than a kiss. But she wanted more, so much more. She wanted to feel his hands on her everywhere, his mouth in places that hadn't been kissed in a long, long time. She wanted to rediscover the joy of being a woman and she wanted him to take her there.

A groan escaped him. His arms tightened. *Yes!*

Then, so fast she nearly stumbled, he let go of her. She forced her eyes open, and saw him looking at her with horror. Horror?

He swore. Then he turned and walked away from her, from the house, and into the deepening night.

What the hell had just happened?

Chapter Seven

Liam stomped off over bare ground, toward distant trees and mountains, spewing every cuss word he knew and maybe even inventing some. How would he know? They tripped off his tongue easily enough so maybe he had just forgotten he knew them.

What he hadn't forgotten was that Sharon was Chet's wife. Widow. What he hadn't forgotten was that he was broken in some important ways and she deserved better. Far better.

"God, Chet," he muttered into the deepening night, "don't hate me, man."

Unfortunately, he didn't think Chet would hate him. So there went that excuse.

He dropped down finally to sit cross-legged in the grass. He could hear a stream's liquid voice nearby but couldn't see it. Closing his eyes, he remembered the nights when he and Chet had sat together in the mountains of Afghanistan, in the dark, talking quietly while keeping watch. Often they had been sitting back-to-back, night-vision goggles giving them a view of the surrounding country, sometimes mountains, sometimes farmland. They were forward posts, partly a net of protection for their fellow soldiers, partly intelligence gathering. Always he and Chet were instantly alert at any movement or unusual sound. At night, sound could carry far.

But they talked, too. Very quietly, in short bursts before returning to silent observation.

"I kissed your wife, Chet. You know that, don't you?"

She's been alone a long time, buddy. I never wanted that for her.

No, Chet hadn't wanted that for her. He'd even felt guilty about it from time to time. Liam could remember those conversations, him trying to buck up Chet by reminding him Sharon knew she was marrying a soldier.

"But it feels different when you're living it," Chet had argued right back. "I married a woman, a good woman, and then I left her alone."

"Duty's a bitch," Liam had replied.

It was. Always. He remembered that much for sure. But he remembered the other times, too, and sitting there in the dark by a stream he couldn't see, he recalled one of them. He wondered if somehow Chet had known that one of those days he was going home in a box.

"I want her to get over me, Liam, if something happens. I want her to move on and have a happy life. I'd never forgive myself if she didn't."

Liam had tried to prod him out of those thoughts.

Thoughts he superstitiously felt could be dangerous. They hadn't happened often, but they'd happened.

"Cut it out, Chet. You're gonna go home and have six kids, and I won't visit because they'll drive me crazy."

Chet had laughed. "Not six. Just two."

Now, not even two. He recalled the conversation earlier with Sharon and realized what she'd been trying to say: there were wounds for everyone because of the war. Many different kinds of wounds.

"Dumb ass," he said aloud. The night didn't argue with the assessment. How could he have gone on about genes and names? That wasn't the point. Having a piece of Chet was the point.

It's okay that you kissed her, he seemed to hear Chet say. *Just don't toy with her.*

"I got nothing to offer her, Chet. I'm a wreck."

Depends on who's looking.

"Damn it," he said to the strengthening breeze. "You always were an optimist."

The stream seemed to laugh. Just as Chet would have laughed.

"It's not funny." Although he supposed it was in a way. Had Chet come home he'd have carried a lot of baggage. War did that to a man. Nobody came home unchanged. So they were all broken, one way or another. Question was, as he had imagined Chet saying, "who was looking."

He sighed, resting his elbows on his knees and opening his eyes. He liked it here. He was having a whole lot less trouble overall with anger and frustration, though it sometimes rolled through him like an unexpected afternoon thunderstorm. He knew a big part of the peace he found here was the quiet. The steady rhythm of work, the few people. He still had trouble being around lots of people. He'd felt it at the diner. Almost like it had become too much stimulation. And he liked being on this ranch, liked the physical labor.

Then there was Sharon. Just as he had about decided that he might never learn to get along with people again, he'd arrived here and found Sharon. She occasionally got annoyed with him, but it blew over, and she didn't seem in any hurry to give him his marching orders, even though he'd been living in expectation of it.

He was still full of rough edges, temper and moodiness. He still sometimes said things he shouldn't. Occasionally, he wasn't even sure he was making sense. But she seemed to find sense in him even when they disagreed, or he said some stupid thing like that business about genes and family names. Even when he didn't get it, she didn't act as if he wasn't smart enough; she just explained it differently.

He didn't feel on edge around her anymore, and he wasn't constantly worrying about saying or doing the wrong thing. She had given him space to be whatever he was.

That was something he was still trying to figure out for himself. The rehab people had tried to make him feel like he had a whole world out here waiting for him, that he'd find his way and a good life. It had sounded good, but he'd known damn well they were ushering him out the door, having figured they'd gotten him as far as they could. Washing their hands of him. Maybe because they had to, maybe because they really couldn't do any more, and there were so many vets in need of them. Still, given all the deficits they'd warned him about, he'd felt something like trash swept to the curb.

Especially with no one and nothing to turn to. He didn't blame his sister anymore, but she was all he had. His parents were long since dead. His buddies, those who were left, had either moved on with their own lives or were still dashing around the globe in uniform. He couldn't just turn up on one of their doorsteps looking for a haven while he sorted himself out.

So he'd hit the road on his mission to deliver the letter that just kept burning a hole in his head and heart. At least he'd had a point and destination, but he'd figured he was going to be up the creek once he delivered that letter.

Wandering, rudderless, unable to even read the packages of food he was buying.

It wasn't self-pity. God knew they'd spent enough time making him aware of what was wrong so that he could be prepared when it slapped him in the face.

But beyond getting that letter to Sharon, the future had been one great big blank.

All of this thinking was giving him a headache. It struck him that he was just trying to avoid the core issue, anyway: his attraction to Sharon. God, he wanted that woman. And even if Chet didn't mind, and even if that whole conversation had played out in his imagination, that injunction remained a good one: don't toy with her.

Wherever those words had come from, he needed to heed them. Good advice. *Watch your step, Liam.*

All of a sudden, Sharon's face floated before his mind's eye, and he remembered how she had looked when he'd abruptly let go of her.

Hell and damnation. He had some fences to mend, though he couldn't imagine how. Maybe he just needed to go back and take his medicine. By now she probably had plenty of things she wanted to say about the way he'd acted.

God, it would be nice if he could stay on track with anything besides painting. Like dealing with a mess he'd just made with a woman he liked, rather than stomping off and leaving her probably feeling like…well, something not nice.

"Back to the house," he ordered himself. If he had to talk to himself every step of the way, he wasn't going to get lost following some other train of thought. "Sharon. Talk to Sharon."

He didn't even want to think about what he probably looked like striding across the fields toward the distant light of the house, mumbling the same words to himself over and over again. At least there was no one to see.

"Talk to Sharon." It was the only guidepost he had right now.

When he got back to the house, he found her in the kitchen sitting at the table with a cup of coffee. She didn't look happy. In fact, she almost glared at him.

For an instant, he wasn't sure why. Then, "Talk to Sharon," popped out of his mouth and he corralled his wandering thoughts again.

"Yes," she said acidly, "by all means, talk to me."

"About what?" Stupid question, judging by the way her mouth dropped open.

"About why you kissed me and then looked like I was an ax murderer."

"You couldn't possibly know that."

She gaped. "Couldn't know what?"

"How someone would look at an ax murderer." As the words slipped past his lips, he had the strong feeling he had just said the worst thing possible. Now he was in for it, but what the hell did ax murderers have to do with this?

Then she astonished him. First, a little sound escaped her, like a small bubble, then she erupted laughing.

Now he was truly perplexed. "What's so funny?"

"You're right. I couldn't possibly know how anyone would look at an ax murderer."

He desperately needed to know something. "Which one of us is talking crazy? Me?"

"Both of us, I think," she said, wiping at her eyes, her voice still breaking on a laugh.

He came farther into the kitchen and she waved him to a seat. "Grab some coffee and sit down."

"I thought you were mad."

"Now I'm not so sure. Didn't you come in saying you wanted to talk to me? So let's talk."

He got the coffee and sat facing her across the table. And like a bomb out of nowhere, he suddenly remembered the way she had felt crushed against him, her mouth open to him, so welcoming and warm. His groin ached and he forced himself to look down before he proved his stupidity once again.

"Why," he managed to ask, "did you think I looked at you like an ax murderer?"

"Because you looked so horrified after you kissed me. It was a great kiss, Liam, but it was just a kiss."

Just a kiss? He didn't know if he liked that, but he quelled a rush of disappointment that maybe she hadn't felt anything like what he'd felt while holding her and kissing her. Best to just listen. His mouth was capable of getting him into a whole lot of trouble.

"What happened?" she asked finally. "Why did you stop kissing me and leave so fast?"

"It wasn't you," he said with certainty. "I'm sorry I made you feel bad."

"So I didn't do something wrong? I didn't repulse you?"

Shock rippled through him. This was worse than he had guessed. "God, no! It was me. Just me. Guilt, I guess."

"Guilt?" Her face seemed to sag a bit. "Chet," she said quietly.

He didn't answer because she was right. Chet. He'd felt a sudden shaft of pain, a fear that he was betraying his friend. His *best* friend. Even though he knew as sure as he knew anything that Chet wouldn't feel that way.

"Chet will always be part of both of us," she said quietly. She ran her finger over the tabletop, drawing an invisible pattern. "Always."

"Yes."

A few minutes passed. *Talk to her.* The command remained with him, but he couldn't figure out what to say. It angered him that he couldn't remember how to deal with this, hated that he sensed he should know how but that some door in his mind was barricaded. With a major effort of will, he stilled the burgeoning frustration. Focus on Sharon. Focus on how to make her feel better.

As if he knew.

"Maybe," she said slowly, "you should read the letter he sent me. The one you traveled so far to bring me."

"That's private."

"Somehow I think you need to read it as much as I did."

Private words. Words his best buddy had intended only for his wife's eyes. He moved uncomfortably on the chair as she rose and went to get it. It felt like trespassing into a place he didn't belong, but it was Sharon's letter now, and if she really felt he should read it...

The limitations on his judgment struck him again. Sometimes he just plain didn't know how to evaluate things, or whether his reactions were the right ones. So maybe he should just go with what Sharon thought was right. If she felt he needed to see that letter, maybe he did.

Maybe he'd find some peace in it. Or some resolution. Even just a simple answer to questions that never quite fully formed in his head.

She returned and handed him the envelope he'd carried so far and for so long, the one stained with blood from his own wounding. A strong wave of emotions ripped through him at the sight of it. Flashes of memory hit him squarely in the heart: watching Chet write this, taking it with some joking about it, then watching Chet laugh as he wrote his own. Finding the letter crumpled in his duffel when he'd recovered his memory. Feeling it like the heaviest of burdens, a duty left uncompleted. The constant ache for a friend lost.

A searing, heart-wrenching, gut-wrenching need that had driven him to take to the road to finish this one last favor for a friend.

"I don't know if I can," he murmured.

She reached across the table. "I'll read it to you."

An old anguish rose in him, eased a little by time, but as familiar as an old shoe. "Sharon..."

She looked at him, her gaze liquid. "All right. He

told me to move on, Liam. He told me that if I didn't, I'd turn his heaven into hell."

God, that sounded like Chet. The garrote of grief cut at his throat, making speech almost painful. "He was amazing."

"In what way?"

He shook his head a little, swallowing repeatedly, trying to ease the ache that strangled him. "He was a good man." Inadequate words. Liam had seen how war twisted some people, but not Chet. "Like helping those farmers and herders." How did he explain what that meant in a place where any man, even one with a herd of goats, could be a mortal enemy? Where you could trust no one, really, except your buddies? But some part of Chet refused to be corrupted.

"I see the same thing in you," Sharon said.

He started to shake his head, but stopped himself. It was an argument he couldn't have simply because he didn't feel capable of arguing such a thing. How would he know what kind of man he was? He knew what he was *capable* of, which was a whole different thing. But Chet had been capable of those things, too. A soldier had to be.

"Are you moving on?" His gift for saying exactly what popped into his head seemed to be still with him. As soon as he heard the question emerge, he realized it might sound exactly wrong, but it was too late. It was out there now, and he tensed, awaiting her response.

"I think I am." Her voice was low, very quiet. "I think I am," she repeated more firmly. "Part of me died with Chet, Liam, but there's still a lot of me left. A lot of life ahead of me. I'm beginning to feel…well, I want goats. I want a piece of that dream we were going to build together, because it was *my* dream, too." She touched the letter that lay on the table, caressing it with her fingertips. "I'll never be able to thank you enough for bringing this to me. I needed to hear him say it." Then she looked straight at him. "You needed to hear him say it, too."

Echoes of the mental conversation he'd had with Chet a little while ago reverberated in his head. But then he'd known Chet almost as well as he'd known himself. When you faced death at a man's side over and over again, you got to know him in ways that really mattered.

"Maybe so," he finally said. Although it was what he would have expected of Chet, she was right. Knowing he'd actually said it to her meant a whole lot to him.

"It was different over there," he said, although he wasn't quite sure why. "We lived faster. Didn't look back too much, didn't look forward any further than we had to. Except every now and then on a quiet night, we'd talk about home."

She listened intently. Then when he fell silent she asked, "I know what Chet's dreams were, mostly, but what were yours?"

"I don't know. Honest to God, if I had any, I don't remember them now."

"That's okay. It wasn't exactly a plan-making situation most of the time."

"Not those kinds of plans, anyway." He thought it over, straining to recall something, anything, because it seemed somehow weird to him that he hadn't had any plans. But a big blank answered him. "I don't know. I just don't know."

"That's kind of where you are now, isn't it?"

The reminder didn't exactly please him, but he couldn't deny the truth of it. "I'll figure something out."

"I know you will. Take your time. I'm happy having you here and you're an incredible help."

That made him feel good enough to crack a small smile. "I'm glad." He liked feeling useful, and it had been a while. A long while. "So I shouldn't feel guilty about wanting you?"

It was a stupid thing to say, but he couldn't help enjoying the way color rose from her collar to flood her face with pink. Or the way she pressed her palms to her cheek.

"You're so blunt," she said.

"I warned you."

Embarrassed as she clearly felt, she still laughed. "Yes, you did."

"If you hate it…"

"Did I say I did? It just takes some getting used to. Most people are more…circuitous. But that's not necessarily a good thing."

"As long as I don't upset you."

"You might have noticed that when you do I let you know." She dropped her hands as her blush faded. "Do you want to work on your reading tonight?"

Her change of direction caught him by surprise, and it took him a moment to follow. He was still getting used to the way things could suddenly shift, but it seemed he was getting a bit better at it. And actually, maybe it was a good thing, because it had been a stressful conversation, the kind of thing that not so very long ago could have sent him on a long walk to avoid the anger or frustration.

"You know what I can't stand?" he asked suddenly.

"What?"

"The way I react to stress and tension now. I used to handle a lot of it."

"I imagine you did. And now?"

"Now I get angry or frustrated, or just walk away."

She hesitated so visibly that he could see it. She had questions she wanted to ask.

"Go ahead," he said. "You have to deal with me. What do you want to know?"

She chewed her lip, then asked, "How much of that is from the injury, and how much from the emotional difficulty of dealing with it?"

"I don't know, Sharon. They weren't clear on that. Or if they were, I sure didn't get it. Maybe they didn't know, either. There's all this stuff that gives me fits right now. Painting the barn is easy. Fixing that door I broke was a sweat. It was like staring right in the face of the things I can't do anymore."

"That would be stressful, all right."

"It's maddening sometimes. But it's reality and I have to learn to deal with all these new limits."

"And maybe discover ways you're not limited. Like painting the barn."

"But I shouldn't be kissing you." Funny, he could lose almost any thought in midtrack without warning, but he seemed to be fixated on that. "It wasn't just guilt about Chet. Yeah, that was a big piece of it. But there was another part, too. I'm broken. I'm too broken to be kissing a woman."

She erupted. "Don't you say that, Liam O'Connor. Don't you even think that. Ever again. Do you understand me?"

He stared into her angry, sparking eyes. "Loud and

clear." For some stupid reason, a smile stretched his face. That didn't make any sense to him, but there it was, and there was no mistaking the feeling on his face. He guessed he liked it when she got mad. It left no question about where he stood with her. "But that doesn't change the facts."

"What facts? All of us have things we can't do."

"I have more than most."

"Well, that depends, doesn't it? On what you want to do, and the ways you can come up with to work around a problem. You worked your way around those directions for fixing the door. Stop thinking about limitations and start thinking about exploring possibilities."

"I'll bet you say things like that to your students."

"Well, yes. Of course I do. Everybody has different abilities and different limitations. Some of my students struggle with basic math. Others struggle with reading, or writing a composition. Some can draw and others can't. That doesn't make any of them less valuable."

Then she utterly astonished him. She rose and came around the table. "Shove back," she said.

So he pushed back from the table. Before he had any idea what she was about, she sat on his lap, wrapped her arms around his neck and looked straight into his eyes. "I want you, too," she said bluntly.

He barely caught his breath before she pressed her mouth to his.

"So take that," she said, the words a warm whisper against his lips before her tongue found his and engaged in a duel he certainly hadn't forgotten.

He was sure this must be wrong for her, but how could something so wrong feel so right? And why was he worrying when she was the one who had initiated this?

But whatever questions he might want to raise swiftly washed away in a rising tide of overpowering desire. His groin ached, his staff stiffened so fast it was almost painful, and her warm rump pressed against it both answered a need and made it stronger.

There was no uncertainty in her kiss. More warmth washed through him as he realized she had meant it: she wanted him, too. This time, no questions about Chet or his own inadequacies speared through the hot fog of desire. Elemental need took over.

He wrapped his arms around her, holding her tight and reveling in being this close to her as much as in the pounding passion she evoked in him. God, it had been forever, and Sharon just made it more special.

But all too quickly, she pulled back. With effort, he opened his eyes, stifling the urge to groan with each little movement she made in his lap.

Her lips looked swollen, her eyes hazy and smiling. "Have we got that straight now?"

Then she slipped off his lap and returned to the far side of the table. He sat stunned and aching, feeling as if he'd just been sideswiped by something huge that he hadn't seen coming. Feeling as if he were a thirsty man who'd just had a glass of water pulled away from him.

Yet it seemed, as the hunger began to subside, that it hadn't been pulled away. Not really. She'd offered something and left it to him to decide. Now? Later? Never?

He might be messed up, but he wasn't so messed up that he didn't sense the dangers here. *Don't toy with her.* Whether the warning was his own or Chet's didn't matter. It was an important warning. This was not a woman he wanted to fool with. Or hurt by taking advantage of her.

He was staring at a minefield, and as the ache eased, he tried to figure out its dimensions. No flings here. No way. But the rest? Was he even remotely ready for something more enduring and deeper?

Hell if he knew. He was still finding his way through the minefield in his head. All he knew was that passion wouldn't be enough here.

Did they have this straight now? The question echoed in his head. Far from it. In fact, he had the feeling matters had tangled up in knots worse than ever.

He had tumbled in over his head.

Chapter Eight

Painting the barn came to a halt. The paint Sharon had chosen was on back order. Everything, Sharon thought, seemed to be on hold. Liam seemed to have withdrawn in some way, probably because she had kissed him, and she couldn't exactly blame him. She wanted him, yes, but this was getting a bit heavy for both of them.

It wasn't just Chet. No. Liam was still struggling to deal with his changed circumstances, and she was just emerging into a world that needed a whole lot of rebuilding in the wake of Chet's loss. Rebuilding she had seriously neglected.

They were a couple of walking wounded, she thought without humor. Liam's withdrawal exhibited more sense than her own behavior. Except, how was she measuring his withdrawal? Just because he hadn't tried to kiss her again?

A little space and a little time on that score would serve them both. She'd been alone too long, and maybe she couldn't trust her judgment. Although she certainly hadn't felt even the least spark of interest in any man before Liam's arrival. No, it was specifically Liam who attracted her, but what did attraction amount to? It was a fleeting thing, an unreliable guide.

She tried to follow his lead. He liked to be busy with his hands, so she made him a list of repairs around the place. He worked his way through it religiously, and when he needed help, he didn't hesitate to ask.

She saw in him, however, a growing confidence. With each task that stymied him, they'd go to her computer, find directions, talk them over, and then she would watch as he steadily organized the steps so he could follow through.

He really wasn't as bad as he thought, except with the reading. He had a command of simpler words, and little by little he began to write again, a word here and there as a reminder. He liked that he could tuck scraps of paper in his pocket and pull them out when he needed to.

Diagrams were easiest for him still, but he definitely was beginning to leave that in the past, relying instead on short written steps, carefully numbered. In short, he was learning, and a man who could learn could do a lot.

His bursts of frustration came less often, although they could still erupt. It remained, however, that she was seeing what she considered to be remarkable improvement.

Part of her wished she had known him before the injury, but another part of her wisely realized that it was probably better for both of them. He did enough of his own self-comparisons, and when he did she could see the frustration build. She felt a pang every single time she heard him mutter, "I ought to know this!"

Anger still simmered beneath his surface, too. That concerned her, but she didn't know how to bring it up, nor was she sure she should. God knew, he had enough to be angry about. As long as he wasn't directing it at her, it wasn't her business. Well, except that it bothered her to see him feeling that way so often.

But she couldn't imagine a cure, or how even talking about it might be useful. Like all his other problems, this was something he had to find a way to deal with himself.

Regardless, he'd done numerous things around the house, things she could have done herself if she hadn't become so disinterested before: a dripping faucet, a running toilet, some splintered baseboard, squeaky doors and one that had needed to be planed. He'd even started working on the porch railing, where some rotting posts needed replacement. That one would take some time as he figured out the steps.

At that moment, he was busy on the interior of the barn. She didn't even want to look at that. There'd been stuff in there when she and Chet had bought the place that they'd never touched, some of which she couldn't even identify, and neither of them had been in any hurry to get rid of things that might eventually turn out to be important.

Her world was full of questions, she supposed. Questions about herself and Liam. But that was an improvement over the months when she had felt either dead inside or so torn by sorrow, she wanted to be dead.

She was getting restless, too. She wanted to do

things, and this holding pattern they seemed to have settled into didn't suit her now.

Making up her mind, she went out to the barn where she found Liam sitting on the fender of an old, rusty tractor, looking around. She was amazed by how much space there seemed to be in here now.

"Wow, you've been busy!"

He cocked his head to one side. "A barn isn't much use if there's no room left to use."

"I'm still amazed. We just left it alone. The task overwhelmed me, and I didn't have a real use for it yet."

"Well, you'll be able to use it now. All it needed was some rearranging."

"And organizing. Do you recognize all this stuff? I sure don't."

He half smiled. "Nope. It'd probably be good to get one of your rancher friends out here to look around. You might not even need half of it, or you might find out it's all important if you get goats and stuff."

"That's why it's all still here." A laugh bubbled out of her. "We were complete tyros at this, Liam. Chet and I would have had quite a learning curve."

"But you still want to get started."

"I do. Listen, I need to get away for a while. I need a change of scenery. Do you want to come to town with me?"

His hesitation was palpable, but then he slid off the fender. "If you don't mind waiting while I clean up. I'm grubby."

She was relieved that he wanted to go. They'd both been locked up inside themselves for too long, and since he'd withdrawn, it had seemed even worse. As she walked back to the house, she wondered how she had survived all the months when she had chosen utter solitude. Yes, she continued her card games with her friends, and teaching had filled a lot of time, but there had been the other times, the holidays, the summer vacation, when she spent days and days talking to no one.

That was definitely not healthy, and maybe it had been the worst possible way to deal with her grief. How many invitations had she turned down at Thanksgiving and Christmas, afraid of the pain she'd feel being among happy families, rather than considering it might have taken her out of herself?

Time for some serious change, she told herself. Heading up the stairs, she changed into fresh jeans and a cotton polo, then listened to the thud of Liam's feet following her, and the sound of him showering.

Downstairs again, she waited patiently and drank a glass of milk to tide her over. Time for a change, indeed, but what kind of change? She needed to talk to Ransom about those goats, for one thing. Find out exactly what she'd be getting into. Maybe she ought to call the vet, Mike Windwalker, and find out what kind of animals he knew of that needed a good home. Maybe goats would be too much to start with.

Seldom had she felt as ignorant as she did right then. A dream, and she hadn't even bothered to study up on it. And she was a teacher? She laughed at herself.

But once there had seemed like all the time in the world to get to things. Life had taught her in the harshest of all possible ways that time wasn't endless, that postponement might well mean never doing something.

Liam joined her and they headed out to her truck. As soon as they were bouncing down the drive to the county road, he asked, "You thinking any more about those goats?"

"I'm thinking it's time I did some research. I'll talk to Ransom, maybe to the local vet about it. Who knows, they might tell me to start with something else. I don't want to get in over my head, or take on something that might be more than I can handle when school starts in the fall."

"I can help you."

Her heart stopped. Was he offering to stay indefinitely? If so, why?

He must have realized how that might sound, because he abruptly added, "If you want me hanging around. If you don't want me to leave, I mean."

"Why would you want to stay?" Then she wished she could call the words back. "That didn't come out right. I mean..." What exactly did she mean?

"It's okay. I stumble into it all the time. I like it here. I like the work. It's peaceful. I'm managing to deal with most of it, I think."

"You are. Splendidly."

"You're easy to be with, too. I met plenty of people after I got out of rehab who weren't easy. Didn't meet anybody I liked, except this one guy."

"What happened with him?" Her heart was tripping fast, although she wasn't sure exactly why.

"Ah, hell, some guys were giving me crap at a gas station when I stopped to get some food. They know when you're not right, you know?"

She hated to hear him say that, hated to hear he felt that way, but bit her tongue to hold the words back and let him talk.

"It was nothing unusual. Three of them started making fun of me, calling me names. I just wanted to get out of there because I was getting mad."

"I imagine so!" And he called that *nothing unusual?* God, she hated to think what he might have endured on his way to her.

"No, you can't imagine what would have happened if I'd lost my temper." From the corner of her eye, she saw his fists clench on his lap. "There's muscle memory, you know? Stuff you don't need your brain to sort out before you act. Plenty of mine is still intact. That's how I painted the barn. Well, I can still fight. The army taught me good, and lots of experience taught me better. If I'd blown my lid with those guys, I'd probably be on my way to prison."

"Oh, Liam."

"It is what it is. I was getting so mad, and I knew I had to just walk away, but they kept following me. I was that close to decking all of them. Hell, I don't know. I might have killed them. So up walks this guy, a trucker, not real big or beefy, maybe in his fifties. He must have seen the patch on my jacket. Anyways, he tells these guys to cut it out, making sport of a wounded vet is a disgrace, and if they weren't ashamed enough to stop maybe the cops could help them."

"Oh, my God." The words slipped out under her breath, and her entire chest tightened. "How can people be so vicious?"

"They just can," he said. "You know that."

She did, but she didn't like it when she saw it or heard about it.

"Anyway, I liked that guy. The three idiots backed off and he offered me a lift on his truck if I was headed west. Nice guy."

"I would say so."

He fell silent, perhaps lost in the memory, and when she glanced his way, she saw his hands were still bunched into fists. Instinctively, she reached out to lay a hand over one of his. She didn't say anything. She figured words were utterly inadequate right now.

She felt something like a tremor run through him, then his hand relaxed beneath hers. A minute later and he turned it over to clasp her hand.

"So what had you been eating? Things from convenience stores?"

"Pretty much. Or fast food. I could remember how to order a burger and fries." He surprised her with a chuckle. "Work-arounds, like you said. I learned a few of them on the road."

To her, it sounded awful, but when she paused to think about it, she had to admit he'd done very well for someone who couldn't read, and admitted he had trouble following through without a list of some kind. He'd made it all the way to her front door.

Then she pondered how it must have impacted him emotionally to be treated that way. No wonder he didn't seem keen on going to town. When she thought of the courage it must take to risk that kind of scene again, her throat tightened. No wonder he was willing to stay at her ranch. There, at least, he didn't face scorn.

A proud warrior brought low in service to his country shouldn't have to face that kind of treatment. She glanced at him again, pained to think of the transformation he had undergone, the transition he had to make to a new and different life. And how many tens of thousands of others were faced with the same changes, the same problems, the same adaptation? She couldn't bear to imagine it.

It was hard enough to see in Liam, and she hadn't known him before. But she had known Chet, had known how capable and confident he'd been in most things. If he were facing this…

She thought she had a pretty good idea of how Chet would have felt about it. How hard it would have been for him to adjust to the fact that he could no longer do things he had once taken for granted. She could well imagine his frustration and anger.

So maybe that was a large part of what Liam was experiencing. Maybe his emotions were driven by a clear-cut delineation, the realization that he was no longer the person he used to be, no longer capable of many things he had once done easily. It would be crazy-making, for her, anyway. The more she thought about it, the more she felt Liam was coping remarkably well.

"Are you up to lunch in town?" she asked. "If not, I'll just run in and pick up something to go."

"I thought…" He paused. "I seem to remember you saying you needed a change of scenery."

"I can get that in a lot of ways. I'm asking if you want to deal with the diner. You don't have to."

"Let's get lunch," he said with a decisiveness that pleased her. Evidently, this was one more hurdle he wanted to get over.

Then he said wryly, "You can always protect me."

She almost laughed because of his tone. "Count on it."

"That's the way I had you figured." Then he sighed. "Let's see how much of that menu I can figure out. You've been working hard enough on my reading."

"You've been doing all the work." As she spoke, she realized how true that was. He *had* been doing all the work. All she'd really done was give him space to figure things out, and a little help from time to time. "I'm not taking any credit for your accomplishments."

Whatever his deficits, Liam had enough strength and determination for any ten people. He just didn't quit. Well, except for the times when he'd walk away because the frustration and anger needed to be contained. But that was a coping skill, too, one that had to be tough.

Summer had reached its peak, and they hadn't had any recent rain. The streets were quiet as they entered town, and seemed almost to be baking under the sun. Maybe Maude's wouldn't be too busy.

No sooner had she stepped inside when she realized she might have made a mistake. A few teachers were there, friends of hers, and they immediately waved her over. She looked at Liam and received a brief nod from him. So he was willing to walk into this with her. Three other women must seem like a mob to him.

"Howdy, stranger," Alice Shepling said, sliding her chair down to make room for them. Cassie Blair, who had recently married a local rancher after coming here from Tampa, also shifted to make more room. Connie Jepson, the eldest of the group by far, studied Liam speculatively.

Sharon introduced him as an army buddy of Chet's, who was helping her out. They welcomed him warmly, and he responded with a nice smile. When the menu came, though, he didn't try to read it. Instead, he ordered exactly what he'd had last time. Nice cover, she thought.

"We're talking about the anti-bullying program

Cassie and Linc started last year," Alice said. "We need to expand it and improve on it. All ideas are welcome." She smiled at Liam, including him in the discussion.

"We had a really bad bullying case last year," Alice went on to explain. "A group of students ganged up on one boy, and by the time we knew what was happening…well, he attempted suicide."

Sharon felt Liam tense beside her. Not the best topic of conversation given what he'd experienced. She started trying to imagine reasons to get up and leave, but they'd already ordered. Damn!

"That's terrible," Liam said quietly.

"It went beyond the student, though," Connie added. "Cassie here was being bullied, too, by a parent who was mad at her for reporting the problem."

"You were bullied?" Liam looked at Cassie.

"Yes. I suppose that's exactly what it was. Although he went beyond what most people would think was bullying."

"He most certainly did," Alice said indignantly. "Threats, property damage and finally an attack on you. And let's not forget that some of the supposed adults around here bullied you a bit, too. It was all very ugly, and could have cost a student his life. Hell, Cassie could have been killed. So we're determined to start a program as early as kindergarten to teach the children that this kind of behavior shouldn't be tolerated."

"Social pressure does a lot," Liam offered.

Sharon was delighted that Liam was joining in and seemed to be relaxing. When Maude slammed his plate down in front of him, he barely twitched a muscle. She was almost ready to jump out of her skin, wondering how this would go.

"Positive social pressure," Connie said. "We don't want it to get negative unless it has to."

Liam simply nodded and began to eat. Sharon dug into her salad, mostly listening to the others while remaining alert for any distress from Liam. He seemed okay, though, listening to everyone, nodding from time to time, and when the conversation drifted on to more mundane things, he appeared to enjoy it. He didn't say much, though. She wondered if he was afraid he'd come out with the wrong thing if he talked too much.

Just as she thought lunch was winding down, and that they'd skated through a minefield fairly well, Alice asked, "Liam, are you home on leave?"

Sharon tensed. She started to answer, but Liam replied first, and bluntly. "Discharged," he said flatly. "Traumatic brain injury."

The gasps came from all around the table. Sharon considered throwing thirty bucks on the table and getting up to leave right then. She looked at her friends, hoping they wouldn't ask too much more, especially since they'd already gotten more than they'd been expecting. Their faces, at first frozen, began to melt into sympathy.

"Oh, my God," said Alice. "I'm so sorry! I can't imagine the hell that must be for you."

"It isn't exactly fun," Liam said. Apparently, he was not going to pull any punches, either because he couldn't or because he didn't give a damn. "I make do. Sharon's a big help."

"She would be," Cassie said quietly.

"Liam's been a big help to me, too," Sharon said quickly. "He painted that whole darn barn for me, and has repaired a bunch of other things."

Alice spoke dryly. "You mean you've finally resurrected the old gray elephant?" She leaned toward Liam. "That place was in terrible shape. In a few more years there'd have been nothing left to paint."

Sharon took the opportunity to redirect by making a joke. "Hey, I liked the silvered wood."

Alice rolled her eyes. "See? She needs rescuing." She winked at Liam.

He surprised Sharon by smiling.

"It was," Alice said, turning back to Sharon, "getting to the point where you might have been able to make a small fortune selling old wood for picture frames."

That set off a gale of laughter and the tension seeped away.

Twenty minutes later, farewells were said, and Liam had been invited to come back to lunch next week. "It's important," Connie said. "We call ourselves the Lunch Bunch, and Sharon used to come all the time. You make sure she comes again."

Then Sharon and Liam were standing alone on the street beside her truck.

She looked at him. "I'm sorry. I didn't mean to drag you into that. Was it too bad?"

"I enjoyed it. You have nice friends."

"I wondered because you were so quiet."

"Since I started coming sideways at things, I've learned that's often best. Look what happened when I mentioned my injury. It was like I threw a stink bomb in the middle of the table."

"Not for long." Thank God.

"So you used to lunch with them every week?"

"When school is out. During the school year it's

one Saturday a month. The group can vary. Sometimes huge, sometimes just a few."

"It's nice."

"Well, I'm still sorry I forgot about it."

"I'm not. And maybe you didn't really forget."

That sparked her temper a bit. "I *did* forget. I knew it would be hard for you to meet so many new people. Maybe stressful. I wouldn't have deliberately walked you into that."

"Maybe not. Or maybe like that shrink in rehab used to tell me, you're smarter than you think. You forget all about it, but at some level you get prodded to do what you need."

"I was fine!"

"I'm sure. You also needed a change of scene and went right back to something you used to love to do. I don't see what's wrong with that."

She started fuming. "I don't like that. If that's what I wanted I could have come to town by myself."

"You could. But maybe that's not all you needed."

"Damn, don't analyze me!"

He surprised her by starting to smile. "Time for me to shut up, I guess. I sure know how to light your fire."

"Sheesh," she said, and unlocked the truck so they could both get in. "I don't need a shrink."

"I'm not saying you do." He slid in and buckled up while she turned on the ignition. "Sorry you were so worried about me. I hope I didn't embarrass you or ruin your lunch."

"Aw, hell," she said. "Don't even think that. You were fine."

"I didn't know teachers cussed so much."

She glared at him, but as she caught the twitch at the corners of his mouth, her annoyance evaporated. "You're a handful," she said finally, on a laugh. "Dang, I can't stay mad at you."

"Good. Where to now?"

Good question, she thought. They were still parked near the diner and Conard City wasn't exactly overrun with amusements. There was a bookstore, but she couldn't think of anything less likely to entertain Liam than that.

"I don't know," she admitted frankly.

"Got a man you can see about a goat?"

He seemed fixed on that, she realized. But then, she'd told him it was a dream of hers. "Yes," she said, decision made. "Let's go see Dr. Windwalker."

As they were driving toward the veterinary clinic and kennels on the edge of town, Liam asked her pointblank, "Did you give up your lunches because of Chet?"

"I wasn't much interested in socializing."

"Maybe you should start them again. You don't have to take me along. A guy at a ladies' gabfest would be kind of a drag."

"They're not that kind of gabfest, and sometimes we have men come. They didn't mind you being there, Liam."

"They didn't seem to."

But now the tongues would be wagging, she thought. Too bad they'd be wagging about something that wasn't even going on. Hanged for a scarlet woman when she was still living like a nun. A giggle escaped her.

"What's so funny?"

She just shook her head. That was something she definitely didn't want to share with him.

"Goats are cool," Mike Windwalker was telling her a short time later. "They're fun, they're curious and they're independent. They can also be a headache with their mischief, but that's part of their charm. Are you thinking of them as pets?"

"Pretty much," she admitted. "I'm in no position to take it up as anything else."

"Then talk to Ransom Laird. He's got a few he keeps mostly as pets, and he's got a couple of kids he might be willing to part with as long as they're not going for meat. He can help you with dietary requirements and care."

"Dietary requirements?"

Dr. Windwalker smiled. "Everything has dietary requirements when it's penned in. Anyway, he'll know the ins and outs better than I do. I mostly see them for immunizations or when they get sick."

After a stop at the grocery for odds and ends, they headed home as the afternoon turned golden.

"Did you get enough of a scenery change?" Liam asked her.

"I did," she answered. "How about you?"

"I enjoyed it. More than I thought I would."

Then he astonished her by reaching out to rest his palm on her thigh. The touch was warm, friendly, not in any way sexual, but rather intimate, as if they were growing closer.

Sexual or not, she found it hard to concentrate on driving with the weight of his hand resting so casually on her leg. It wasn't getting any better, she realized as warmth began to pool between her legs. No better at all.

At some level she apparently had thought that if she could just ignore the attraction she felt for him, it would go away. The couple of kisses they had shared had been just kisses, and when he had made no further move, she assumed that much as he said he wanted her, he'd made up his mind on the subject.

Now she wondered, and wondering broke down all the walls she'd been trying to build. She was no fool. She knew she'd been alone for a long time. She knew she might be susceptible for reasons that had nothing to do with Liam and everything to do with her. In short, she might be weak and unable to choose what was best for her.

But she realized as they steadily approached her ranch that she hardly cared any longer. She was tired of trying to quash normal needs and feelings out of some misguided sense of…what?

She didn't even really know why she was fighting it so hard, suppressing her longing as much as possible. What was she afraid of? That a brief fling could wound her irrevocably? That Liam might move on and leave her grieving yet again?

That last question caused her to stiffen. That was it, wasn't it? She was afraid of living. Afraid of risking a repeat of the pain of losing Chet. She was sublimating entire parts of herself in the hopes of avoiding pain.

Was that any way to live?

The question nagged at her almost as much as an almost breathless sense of anticipation. She had to fight to keep her eyes on the road, but Liam's hand, heavy on her leg, seemed to have become the focus of her universe. Did that touch mean something? He didn't touch casually, she had noticed. Maybe because of all his years in the army. Maybe because he wasn't a touchy-feely kind of person.

But it remained that other than a kiss, this was the first time he had deliberately touched her. It felt freighted with meaning. Had he reached some decision? She hoped he had, even as she wasn't sure she had herself.

What was she getting into here, anyway? She liked Liam, of that she was sure. And sometimes she wondered if she didn't care for him a little more than that, because of the way she ached for him when he struggled with his frustrations and limitations.

Was she sure she just wasn't feeling overwhelming sympathy? That could be dangerous. But as soon as she tried to think about it, she knew that wasn't it. Maybe in the first few days, but not now.

There was nothing pitiable about Liam. She'd figured that out. He hadn't quit trying, even though he had plenty of excuses to. In the right setting, he was still perfectly competent, and she was finding that his cognitive impairment didn't trouble her at all. She was getting used to it and didn't feel, as she had initially feared, as if he constantly needed guidance.

She'd watched his confidence grow as he'd attacked various jobs and found that he could either still do them, or could figure out how to do them, sometimes with a little help. And it had been rewarding for both of them.

But where did that get her? That she wanted him for the right reasons, or that she wanted him for the wrong reasons? Maybe she needed some time to sort out her own tangled emotional skein before she got into something she might not be ready for.

But wanting was not the same as loving. She knew that to her very core. She had loved once, and she wouldn't mistake desire for that deep and enduring emotion.

So what was she really afraid of? That she might discover that parts of life could still be beautiful?

Another wave of grief for Chet passed through her, quieter now than before. He had missed so many of the good things, and now he would never know them.

You'll turn my heaven into hell.

Chet's loving heart hadn't wanted her to crawl into a grave with him. He didn't want her to deny herself the things he couldn't have. He wanted her to enjoy all of them, even though he couldn't be with her.

That was true love. No, she wouldn't mix it up with anything else, of that she was certain.

They turned onto the dirt drive that led to the house. The barn, whitened with primer, seemed bright against the surrounding countryside, almost like a beacon.

Liam had done that for her. Whether from gratitude or some sense of obligation, didn't matter. He had a big heart, too, and was struggling with demons she could only imagine. But he fought on, determined to make some kind of future for himself. Determined to become as functional as possible. Even the reading lessons spoke volumes. She wouldn't have blamed him if he'd been insulted. A lot of men would have been, feeling it was an attack on their manhood. Not Liam. He'd accepted it and taken to it like a man thirsty for knowledge.

His hand was still on her thigh and it was all she

could think of. Her distracting thoughts were giving way to an awareness of Liam: his touch, his scent, his nearness. It was like being wrapped in a spell of some kind, and she feared it would end as soon as she parked.

She didn't want it to end. She wanted it to go on and on. She wasn't sure how far she wanted it to go, but she knew how much she needed even little things.

God, it had been so long since she'd been touched. So long since she'd been held close for any but the briefest moments of sympathy. She had felt Liam's arms around her, powerful and sure, and she wanted that feeling again.

"I'll get the groceries," Liam said as the truck stopped beside the house. His hand vanished from her leg and she felt the loss as acutely as if a piece of her skin had ripped off.

Fantasies. Just fantasies. He had his own reasons to be cautious about this, too. And she supposed she should be grateful since it seemed her own willpower was dying a rapid death in the face of deeply rooted yearnings.

She left him to get the few grocery bags, no more than he could carry with a single hand, and headed inside, telling her body to calm down, telling herself to banish the disappointment. The touch may have meant nothing. He might have simply rested his hand on her because he was as hungry for human contact as she was.

Considering the glimpses she'd had of his journey to see her, she could certainly understand that. Months in rehab followed by a road trip that had to have stressed him to the max, and all of it alone. In their different ways, they had both been to hell and were just starting to make their way back.

Affection, sorely missed, was as much of a need as any. Maybe that was what they were seeking.

Standing at the kitchen window, looking out, she heard his heavy tread as he walked into the room behind her. Bags rustled as he placed them on the table. She was afraid to turn around and look at him, for fear he might have withdrawn again into that place that had taken him so far away the past few days. Lost in memories? Lost in thoughts about a future? Or simply lost in dealing with his own changes? She had no way to know, and he didn't seem inclined to talk.

She heard him put things in the fridge, and still she didn't move. She tried to focus on her dinner plans, but kept getting sidetracked by thoughts of him, so near and yet so far.

Without warning, powerful arms wrapped around her from behind, causing her to gasp. Warm breath caressed her neck, then his husky voice said, "Did I do something wrong?"

"Oh, no!" She hated to think he was misinterpreting her pensiveness, but how else could he take it when she wouldn't even look at him? "I was just thinking."

He didn't release her. Instead, she felt him settle into his stance more comfortably, legs spreading, and then he drew her back against his chest.

"I know that place," he said. His breath now whispered warmly against her ear. "Lost in thought."

She tried to lighten the moment in defiance of the hot pool of hunger that had settled between her thighs. Damn, it felt as if every cell in her body had sprung to sudden life. She could even feel her nipples pebbling, hoping for a touch. "Did you find any answers to cosmic questions?"

"If you're a cosmic question, then no."

She caught her breath. "Liam…" His name seemed to bear the weight of every burgeoning desire she felt.

"I can't promise a thing," he said. "Do you understand that? I don't know how well I'll deal with who I am now. I don't know for sure that I've got anything to offer."

"I'm not asking for forever here." She wasn't. She was fairly certain of that.

"Good. Because I'm not sure I can give it."

She sighed and let her head tip back against his shoulder. "We're adults," she said pointlessly.

"Which means we can make some really big mistakes."

That made twice today that his insight had startled her. Deficits? What deficits? The important things still seemed to be a part of him. Like that business about her unconscious taking her to town and into Maude's diner, knowing at some level that she'd run into her friends. She didn't want to be analyzed, but he'd hit that nail squarely on the head. Her irritation had come from being so transparent to him, but not to herself.

"I don't know what we're doing here," he said honestly. But then he was always honest, sometimes painfully so. "Do you?"

"No," she admitted. "I just know that resurrection is a hard thing to do."

"That's a good word for it." Then, "Aw, hell."

He turned her around until she faced him, then without a word slid his hands down to cup her rump. As he started to lift her, she instinctively grabbed his shoulders. In one easy movement, he lifted her onto the counter and came to stand between her legs.

"Just a little," he murmured, "just a taste."

She didn't know whether he was talking to her or himself, but it ceased to matter as his mouth found hers.

The melting inside her was instantaneous. She wouldn't have believed that the mere touch of his lips could turn her so soft, relaxing every tension, turning her into a warm puddle.

Like a butterfly seeking nectar, his lips and tongue brushed gently against hers, so gently it was almost maddening when she wanted so much more. Wrapping her arms tighter around his shoulders, she tried to urge him closer, to communicate how much more she wanted.

"Easy," he whispered, though once again she couldn't tell if he was reminding himself or asking her. It didn't matter. Something deep and strong was building in her, and she wasn't going to do one single thing to shatter this moment.

So she remained patient as he tasted her lightly, explored gently. She'd never had a kiss like this, so free of demand, as if asking and almost uncertain. But when his tongue at last slipped between her lips, every cell in her body responded.

Heat swamped her in shimmering waves. Their tongues dueled as if this caress were the ultimate satisfaction. Such a kiss!

Then his hands, which had been resting at her waist, moved. One of them slipped around, tugging her shirt up, slipping beneath it until she felt his calloused palm against the bare skin of her midriff. Warm, rough, yet so gentle. His other hand pulled her closer, even as he moved in to press himself to the throbbing heat between her thighs.

She wanted more and her body signaled it, arching to press tighter to him, lifting her legs to wrap them around him. She felt open, soft, hard and hungry all at once. Heat bloomed throughout her. Breaths came in gasps.

She felt her bra clasp twist, her breasts immediately spilling free of confinement. Then his hand found her there, too, brushing against her nipple over and over while he continued to plunder her mouth.

She felt caught on an arc of fire, sizzling, electric jolts zapping from her mouth to her core, from her breast to her core. The pool of heat between her thighs turned to a heavy, hard ache, clenching and unclenching in time to his rapacious tongue.

She felt his hips rock against hers, felt the hardness of him through all the layers of denim. The pounding in her blood grew deafening, and she dug her fingers into his shoulders needing some purchase as she spun free of gravity.

Then his fingers pinched her nipple and she cried out, throwing her head back. The wave took her now, like a tsunami in its power. His kiss was gone, but immediately replaced by something even more powerful.

As she arched backward, he supported her with his arm, while his other hand continued to toy with her breast, driving her to the edge of insanity. Then she felt the whisper of cool air, but before she had time to really notice it, his mouth clamped over her breast, sucking strong and hard.

Her head bumped the cabinet above, but she barely noticed. She was riding a wild stallion at full gallop, and nothing could halt the cascade of hunger inside of her.

With each pull on her breast, with each lash of his

tongue on her tingling nipple, the undeniable rhythms in her pounded ever more strongly.

Their hips met, again and again, the throbbing ache grew bigger and bigger. It was almost teasing with so much clothing in the way, enough and yet not enough, but what was happening inside her was not teasing. It was real, vital and explosive.

She needed this. Oh, how she needed this. She was flying now, higher and higher, even as the throbbing within her approached a painful crescendo.

All of a sudden, everything inside her exploded. For an instant, her brain emptied of everything but the acute awareness of a satisfaction that was almost excruciating in its intensity. Then, like a spent firework, she shattered in blazing embers of completion.

Chapter Nine

Liam held her close. She could hear his ragged breathing in her ear, and she supposed hers was every bit as ragged. Her heart pounded its way slowly to a calmer rhythm. The throbbing of her body eased slowly, almost reluctantly, as if it were ready to start again.

She heard him draw a long, shaky breath, felt a tremor pass through him. Time had ceased to have meaning, and she didn't know how long it was before he spoke.

"I think I said a taste."

It was certainly more than a taste, she thought hazily. She leaned into him, enjoying his arms around her, enjoying the closeness she had missed for so long.

There was no understanding of how important it was to be this close to another human, to be wrapped in strong arms, unless you had gone without it forever.

It felt like forever since last someone had held her this way.

Not that she would have wanted just anyone to hold her this way. No, it mattered that it was Liam, and that realization niggled at her mercilessly. Then she shoved it away, refusing to cede this time and these feelings to the harsh light of reflection. That could come later.

"Wow," he murmured into her ear. "Just wow."

"Wow," she agreed, burying her nose in his neck, inhaling his particular musky scent mixed with soap and shampoo. He smelled so good to her.

He ran his palms over her back, then surprised her by lifting her and holding her close.

"My legs feel like rubber bands," he said. "You drained me, woman."

The comment elicited a quiet laugh from her as the world spun and he headed for the living room. A half minute later they were settled on the sofa, she straddling his lap, all without separating an inch.

She leaned against him, enjoying the way he rubbed her back. She'd have been happy to stay like this forever. For a while, it seemed he would, too.

Companionable silence, human closeness. It couldn't get much better.

But then her stomach growled noisily. He laughed quietly. "You need to eat."

"I need to make dinner," she admitted.

"I don't suppose there's a pizza delivery service out here."

"Dream on." She laughed reluctantly and sat up even more reluctantly. "I need to cook."

"Maybe we can scrounge something from the fridge. Or find something easy."

"I planned on easy for tonight. I hope the gas grill still works, but I figured I'd make some hamburgers."

"That sounds really good. What can I do?"

"Pull the grill away from the house and take the cover off it. I hate dealing with that."

She eased off his lap, feeling as if she were making a big sacrifice. It wasn't easy, but she supposed it was necessary, especially as a hunger pang struck her. Her lunch salad hadn't stuck around for very long.

Or maybe, she thought impishly, Liam had helped her work up an appetite.

Standing near the kitchen window, she quickly made hamburger patties for them, then started slicing tomatoes and onion, and washing a few lettuce leaves. He had no trouble pulling the grill out to the place she'd indicated, but when it came to dealing with the heavy, waterproof cover, he seemed at a loss once he'd pulled it off.

She paused in her preparations and waited while he studied the cover. He probably felt he should fold it, but couldn't figure out how. She hoped he wasn't getting frustrated.

Just as she was about to drop her knife and go out to help him, something must have clicked for him. He began folding the material, although far from neatly. Maybe he'd decided that any old fold would do for now. It certainly would. In fact, he hadn't needed to fold it at all.

Watching him was a thrill, though, because it called to mind the minutes just past when he had held her in those incredibly strong arms and had showed her that a very essential part of her was alive and well after being repressed for so long.

Man, that had been delicious. But even as remembered sensations began to flood her anew with warmth and a desire for more, warning flags started popping up.

It was all well and good to acknowledge that she'd been trying to avoid pain for a long time now, that she'd pulled out of much of life because she feared close connections and the devastation that could follow when they were lost. It was entirely another to try to delude herself into thinking that didn't matter.

Of course it mattered. Any reasonable adult would know that. To risk such pain again, the reward would have to be great, indeed, and Liam had been quite frank about not being able to promise her anything. He was justified in that. Hell, he hadn't sorted himself out yet, and she, apparently, hadn't sorted herself out, either.

They were both on a dangerous transitional cusp here: he was working his way into a new life, and she was coming out of a long period of grief. In short, they were easy pickings for an easy answer to it all.

She sighed, arranging the lettuce, onion and tomatoes on a plate. Okay, no easy answers, no heedless slip into a relationship that could wound one or both of them. Neither one of them merited the pain if only one of them should become deeply involved. And given their current situations, it might be too damn easy to get involved, for comfort and companionship, if nothing else.

God, she thought, life had been so much easier when she had fallen in love with Chet. None of these daunting questions, just an easy tumble into the most wonderful ocean of human emotions. No knotty questions, just a growing surety.

Life had taken that ease and certainty away from her by teaching her that love could be painful, too. Every bit as powerfully painful as it was wonderful. If that was wisdom, she wished she'd never had to learn it.

She cooked the burgers on the grill, taking her time because Liam seemed interested in how to light it.

"I never had a gas grill," he announced. "When I was a kid it was always charcoal."

"We went with this because it's useful when the power goes out in the winter. If the wind isn't too strong and you can stand the chill, there's a lot you can cook rather than burning the house propane, which we need for heat."

"Does it go out often?"

"The power? Often enough. At least once a winter it'll go out for long enough that I'll be carting food *outside* to keep it cold."

She glanced at him. "I bet you got used to living without any power at all."

"Sometimes. We had generators at some of our forward bases so it would depend on where we were and what we were doing."

"Rugged living."

"No more rugged for us than the people who live there."

"That's a good point. I guess I'm pampered."

He didn't answer, and when she looked up he was staring into space. Oh, God, had she just sent him back to Afghanistan? But then he seemed to shake himself, and the next thing she knew he was smiling at her.

He didn't answer her comment though, and she let it lie.

They let a lot of things lie that evening. The intimacy

had dispelled, and the distance was back. They ate at opposite sides of the table, they watched a comedy on DVD, which didn't seem to interest him a whole lot, and when bedtime approached he went up alone.

The barriers were back in place, leaving her feeling bereft. Later, in her own room, she tossed and turned until finally she gave up and went to sit by her window.

Seated in a valley, the ranch didn't give the longest views as the mountains seemed to rise quickly to the night sky. The moon silvered everything and seemed to invite memory to intrude.

She had spent more nights sitting alone at this window than she could count. Chet had been gone for most of their marriage, and this little easy chair had been a lonely haven for a long time.

Although she had been used to long bouts of solitude, the loss of Chet had been no less painful. Purpose had left her life, and along with it the familiar and much cherished task of writing him every single day about some little thing. She knew from his responses that he often went without mail for a long time, then would receive a whole packet of her letters. He called those times his "real payday."

Planning had deserted her, too, along with dreams for the future. She'd begun running like an automaton, the color leached from her life as surely as the night leached it from the day.

Now she felt the color seeping back into its place, dreams were stirring, however small, and the memory of her lovemaking with Liam, however limited it had been, curled up in her heart with warmth.

If he called that a "taste"....

She almost shivered at the memory of how much he

had aroused her and satisfied her with so little contact. She ought to feel guilty, but no guilt arose in her.

But there would be pain, she thought. It seemed impossible to her that waking the woman in her after all this time could have no price.

Then another thought occurred to her, and that was when the pain pierced her. She had known what she was getting into when she married Chet. In all their years as husband and wife, she had enjoyed only a few months of time with him. Yes, duty called him, and sometimes she suspected that he went right back when he could have taken a tour stateside.

It was never discussed; she didn't know if her suspicions were true. They probably weren't, but their very existence told her something. In her heart she believed that Chet had valued his duty over her. The whole time he was home, talking with her about their future together, still far down the road, she knew he was worrying about his buddies. It had slipped out at times, and while she considered it a mark of the good man he had been, she had sometimes resented it.

Oh, God! When he was home, part of him had still been over there. Had she ever really had his full devotion? She tried to argue the ugly question away. Of course she had. As much as any person had the right to expect from another.

But it remained that their marriage, if counted in actual time living as husband and wife, had been very short. It hadn't seemed so bad when she had been looking forward to when he got out of the army, but looking back... Looking back, she had been cheated. They had both been cheated. Hell, Liam and Chet had spent more time together by far.

Anger burst in her, flooding her with its acid. They'd never had a normal married life, only the pretense of one. Really. A honeymoon once every year, and gaping holes filled in by letters and Skype. She'd lived with it at the time because Chet would have retired at twenty years, and by the time he had died there had only been about six years left. Or maybe the war would end and he'd come home.

Only he hadn't made it home and she felt furious and cheated and even a little deluded. It had been more fantasy than reality.

Jumping up, she climbed into jeans and a sweatshirt. She hurried downstairs, pulled on her boots and a warm jacket, and hurried out the back door, wanting to run, but smart enough even in her anger to realize the dangers of tearing across uneven ground.

"Cheated." She said the word aloud as she stomped her way through the chilly night, across grasses that were already yellowing despite the rain they'd had not long ago.

"Cheated." She said it again, as pain began to intertwine with fury into an agonizing knot. Thank God she hadn't had a child. Chet would have missed the first tooth, the first step, the first word. He'd have missed it all, been a stranger to his own child.

In some ways a stranger to his own wife.

"Damn it!" She swore. She swore for all the other spouses, thousands of them, who had gone through this. For all the sacrifices made to feed the maw of war. For all the pain and loneliness, loss and suffering. And for what?

God, she wished she had a good answer. With a price so high, shouldn't there be an answer?

Ripped by shattering anger and pain, she fell to her knees and pounded the cold ground with her fists. Each hammering blow felt good, releasing the unvoiced anger and perhaps some of the pain.

Then, out of nowhere, she felt a heavy hand begin to rub her back. She gasped, jerking upright and saw Liam kneeling beside her.

"I know," he said. Then before she could ask what he knew, he sat cross-legged and lifted her onto his lap as if she weighed nothing.

"Why?" she gasped as heavy tears began to fall. "Why?"

He wrapped his arms around her and began to rock them both gently. "It's okay," he murmured. "Just cry all you need to."

"But why?"

"It was our duty."

"That's not good enough!"

"Sometimes that's all you have."

She turned her face into his shoulder and wept hard and long. She didn't ask again, just let the last of the grief work its way through her. Somewhere deep inside she knew she was letting go of something, and the letting go felt like tearing her heart out by the roots.

Ages later, exhaustion began to dry her tears, and the pain and anger began to ease.

He began to talk quietly. "We had a duty. We believed in our mission, to help the local people. Sometimes it wasn't easy, but we believed in it, anyway. Sometimes the world seemed to go mad, but we kept right on believing. If you know nothing else about Chet, know this. He never once stopped believing that we were trying to make the world a better place. Some people sneer at that, but they don't matter. We believed, and we tried."

"Yes." Her voice emerged raw and thick after all the sobbing.

"If we were misused or misled, history will decide. But we believed."

"But look at the price!"

"There's always a price. We knew that. So did you."

His words sank into her heart like a stone. Yes, she had known that, but foolishly had believed that she and Chet wouldn't pay it. She'd lived in denial, a fantasy world.

"All we had," she said brokenly, "all we had out of seven years were a few months together. We weren't even together long enough to have a good fight."

"Maybe that's a good thing. I don't know. At least you don't have any bad memories of him."

That much was true, but she had memories of the aching loneliness when he was away. The dissatisfaction that she always tamped down. The need for a fuller marriage, never acknowledged.

"I needed more."

"I suspect he did, too."

"I don't think I even really knew him."

"You knew the man who loved Sharon. That part was for you and you alone."

A shudder passed through her, and the last of the tension inside her slipped away. She melted within the circle of Liam's arms, exhausted.

A long time passed. The chilly air was beginning to penetrate him, and Liam wanted to get her back to the house. He didn't want to disturb whatever she was working through, though.

God, it hurt to see her like this. He knew the holes in his own heart, the loss of too many buddies, Chet foremost among them, but he couldn't plumb the depths of loss she must feel. Or the anger.

"We never had a real marriage."

The words stunned him. He had absolutely no idea how to respond.

She struggled a bit against him and he let her go, watching her rise. He remained seated as she paced in circles in front of him. "It was a dream, Liam. It was a fantasy, castles in the air. We kept right on building them, all of them tagged with *someday*. Someday we'll do this or that. When I retire, we'll do that. Over and over again, we built those castles, cherished them, believed in them and the time never came, Liam. It never came!"

"No." It was the most he dared say, spoken only to let her know he was listening. His chest had grown tight, and he'd have given anything to make her feel better. But he couldn't do that. She had to do it for herself. For once he didn't feel savage frustration because he couldn't do something. All he felt was sorrow.

His arms felt empty without her. He rose, waiting patiently for whatever would come next. Life had taught him how to wait.

"I feel cheated." Her words shook him, but again he said nothing. He could well understand why she felt that way.

Then she pivoted sharply to look at him. "I must sound like a whiner. I talk about being cheated, but look at what you've lost. You've been cheated, too."

"It happens."

"Yeah, it happens. And I'm not the only widow to come out of this mess. Tens of thousands around the world right now."

"The problem," he said carefully, "is that each experience is individual, and it isn't any easier because you can point to so many others who've had the same losses."

"God, Liam, I'm so angry! I'm not even sure I'm being fair about this."

"Fair?"

"To myself or Chet. To what we had. But I know one damn thing for sure. If I ever marry again, I want a real, full-time marriage. I want someone who's there every morning when I wake up, and every night when I go to bed. No more castles in the air."

She started walking toward the house and he followed along.

He spoke. "All the castles we build are in the air."

She stopped short and faced him. "Really? *Really?*" Then the hiccup of a sob escaped her.

"Nobody can ever be sure tomorrow will come."

"No." Her voice emerged as tight as a violin string, the sound drawn out. He resisted the urge to hug her, once again waiting.

"What about you?" she asked.

"What about me?"

"Are you going to build castles in the air again?"

"It seems important. But first I want a foundation. You and Chet had a foundation."

She remained silent for an eternity, then answered quietly, "Yes, we did."

Then she headed for the house.

"I can't sleep," she said as they walked in the back door. "I want some hot chocolate. You?"

"Yes, thanks."

They hung up their jackets on the pegs in the mudroom and she slipped off her boots. He noted that her hands trembled as she pulled out the pan and ingredients. This was far from over.

He understood how grief worked. Hell, they'd laid it out for him more than once during his recovery so he'd have some way of gauging his reactions and feelings. She needed the anger as much as she had needed the weeping. Nor was grief, they had warned him, something that just went away. It eased with time, but spurts of anger and pain would return for a long, long time.

She'd had no help with these feelings. No one to talk to about them. No sounding board. In that respect, he'd been far luckier, having plenty of people at the clinic to listen to him rant about his losses, about what had happened to him. He'd had to grieve for himself as much as for Chet and the others. They'd helped him and encouraged him.

He wished he could do the same for Sharon.

"I feel awful for feeling cheated."

He looked at her back, thinking how slender and delicate she looked. He had to remind himself that she had survived a lot and was stronger than she looked.

"You *were* cheated," he agreed flatly. There it was again—his damned inability to curb his mouth—but he didn't try to call the words back because they were true.

She turned from the stove and looked at him. "It sounds awful."

"That doesn't make it any less true. A lot of military marriages break up because duty comes ahead of everything, even family. Because, like you said, you only had a few months with Chet over a period of years. It's a strain."

"On him, too."

"No doubt. But maybe it's harder at home. More fear and uncertainty because you don't know what's going on. Regardless, your marriage got the short end of the stick. Just a simple fact."

Her eyes seemed to glisten again as she returned to mixing the hot chocolate. He stared at her back, feeling like a ham-fisted lug.

"You know," he said, "I spent most of my adult life dealing with other soldiers, men for the most part. I'm not good with women, so if I step in it, just tell me."

"I have before."

He couldn't deny that.

"I'm not really a different species, you know."

To his relief, he heard a spark in that statement that sounded as if she were edging away from her anger. Not that she wasn't entitled to it. He'd never thought about it before, but she was right. She *had* been cheated. Not deliberately, not by a con, but by life. "The thing is," he said, "it's just life. Life isn't fair, it cheats us, it wounds us, and then all we can do is pick up the pieces. Easy to say, hard to do."

"You've got a lot of pieces to pick up yourself."

"Yeah. So? It just is. I keep telling myself that. Doesn't always work, but it's still true. You've seen me get mad and frustrated more than once. I feel ham-handed, I say things I probably shouldn't, I sometimes can't hold a thought from one minute to the next..."

"You seem to be doing pretty well right now."

"Thanks. But it's still there, the grasshopper in the

brain. Hell, the only reason I haven't been more frustrated is that when I butt up against something I should know how to do and can't remember, you give me just a little push in the right direction. Well, you're helping me. What help have you had, Sharon?"

"My friends..."

"How much have you been seeing them? I bet you've stayed away more often than not because you were afraid. Kind of like I've been hiding from people myself. I don't like being reminded that my head is broken. Why would you want to be reminded of what you've lost?"

He saw her stiffen and pressed his lips firmly together. There he went again, saying things he shouldn't. What did he know, anyway? They'd had a few weeks together, hardly enough to really know anything. He certainly hadn't been able to see how she handled the months after Chet's death.

"Damn you, Liam. You see right through me."

He didn't know how to take that. Frustration rose in a burst and he stood up. Damn it, he couldn't even talk to another person without saying something wrong.

"I'm taking a walk," he said shortly.

She whipped around from the stove. "No, you don't. You sit right down there and talk to me."

"But..."

"I don't care how damn frustrated you're getting. Express it here. Because, damn you, I need your help right now."

"What good will it do if I start yelling about things?"

"I'm not the only one with a right to anger. Now go ahead, yell all you want, and I'll yell right back. You have every right to your frustration and you shouldn't have to go find a corner to hide in when you feel it. The way I did for so long. You're sitting here suggesting I handled it all wrong, so maybe you are, too."

"I didn't say that!"

"Not exactly. But you're right. I went into hiding, for all the good it did me. I don't give a damn if you punch a hole in a wall, but don't walk out on me now."

The woman had steel in her, more than he'd guessed. He returned to his chair, sitting on the edge of it while frustration and anger of his own tingled along his nerve endings.

A few minutes later, she brought mugs of cocoa to the table and sat facing him. "So we just have to start putting the pieces back together."

For a few seconds he had trouble figuring out what she meant, then he remembered what he had said earlier. "I guess so."

"Where do we start, Liam? Where are you going to start?"

"Right here, I guess. If you don't mind. Because I'm feeling better here than I have since I was wounded. I'm remembering things I can do. I'm learning other things."

"Good. I'm still amazed that you made your way out here all alone and facing all that ugliness from idiots. I'm touched. And I'm not sure I could have done it."

"You could have," he said with certainty. "You're tough. And you could have avoided some of the problems I had."

"Because I can remember how to read?"

"And other things. I took a few wrong turns."

"You got lost?"

"Yeah." He clenched his hands and forced them to

relax. "I never got lost in the mountains of Afghanistan, but I got lost on the roads at home."

"But you had GPS back there."

"Not always. Equipment breaks. Even the hardened stuff they gave us. But yeah, I got lost and when I got lost, I got mad."

"So what did you do?"

"Asked people. I told you about a couple of trouble-makers, but most people were nice and even helpful."

"I should hope so. And you have no family?"

He didn't want to go there. He might have accepted it, but that didn't mean it didn't still sting. "My sister. She washed her hands of me as soon as she heard about the extent of my injuries. Can't say I blame her, considering at the time I couldn't remember anything and couldn't even feed myself. Who'd want to take that on?"

Her faced saddened. "Have you tried to get in touch with her?"

"Why? She doesn't need a problem like me. She's got three little kids and a job. Can you imagine her having to explain weird Uncle Liam to young kids? I don't think so. And what if I went ballistic? There's always that chance when I get frustrated."

"You're taking that awfully well."

"I didn't at first." Nor did he want to remember the fury he'd felt that his only living kin didn't want him. It had taken him a while to get to acceptance. "She didn't see any more of me than you saw of Chet, and with me it was since I was eighteen. I'd go to visit her for a week when I was on leave, but I spent the rest of the time kicking around. She didn't really want me around for long, even back then."

"And your parents?"

"Long gone thanks to a drunk driver. What about you?"

"Only child. I avoid my parents these days. They retired to Arizona, Mom's a nasty alcoholic and my dad is one angry man. I can take them for a couple of hours, max."

It was a pretty dismal picture for both of them, he thought. He missed his buddies, and he suspected she'd been missing her friends. They both lacked families, although from what he'd seen, that wasn't always a bad thing.

Regardless, they were two souls cast adrift by loss and they needed a way back to shore.

"Any ideas," she asked, "how we move forward?"

He shook his head, the frustration surging in him again. "How the hell would I know? You're asking the wrong guy, lady. I'm still trying to put myself back together. I can't think much further than the next step right now. What about you?"

"I feel like I'm coming out of a long, dark tunnel. It hurts sometimes. But you're helping."

"Are you talking about the sex we had earlier? Because if you were, don't. It was just sex."

"Just sex?" She hopped up from the table, fury blazing in her eyes. "If that's all you think it was, Liam O'Connor, you can leave right now."

He listened to her run up the stairs and slam her bedroom door. Well, that had really cut it. Count him seven kinds of idiot.

He looked toward the door where she had vanished, fighting an urge to smash something.

Never had he hated the man he had become as much as he did right then.

* * *

Just sex? Sharon paced her bedroom in fury. *Just sex.* No way. It had been something more, and it had torn the shell around her heart wide-open, exposing raw nerves she hadn't even been aware of. And no matter what Liam said, after the way he'd held her afterward and comforted her later out in the field, she figured it wasn't just sex to him, either.

Or maybe she was building another castle in the air, she thought bitterly. She seemed to be good at that. Did that one act imply permanence? No, she wasn't that foolish, but two hearts had touched, however briefly, and to hear it dismissed as *just sex* was maddening.

After the glow had worn off and the night had brought solitude, she'd come face-to-face with some very painful, possibly ugly feelings in herself. Liam was right, she *had* known what she was getting into when she married Chet. She had married a soldier, after all.

The problem was, knowing in advance and actually experiencing it had turned out to be two different things. She supposed that was a basic truism of life, but at the beginning, while she had known it would hurt when he was away, she hadn't guessed how much she'd eventually come to resent it. There was nothing like actual experience to wipe away rosy imaginings.

But *just sex?* Fury seethed in her. She'd been ripped wide-open by the experience, laid naked to all her games and delusions and pretenses by the simple, straightforward reawakening to her own vitality, and he could dismiss it like that.

God! Had that been all it had meant to him? A quickie in the late afternoon? No earth-shattering, gut-wrenching realization that life could be good again? That maybe it could be even better?

She heard the knock on her door and wanted to ignore it, but she knew this house well enough to know that he had been able to hear her pacing. No chance he would think she was asleep.

"What?" she demanded querulously.

The door opened and the man himself stood there. "That came out wrong."

"Oh, really?" She folded her arms and glared at him. "I get that you can't promise a future, but don't you dare dismiss something so wonderful and intense as *just sex*."

"I didn't mean it that way, Sharon. Honest to God."

"Then how did you mean it? Explain it to me, Liam. I'm listening."

"Help me here," he said after a moment. "I'm not saying it wasn't wonderful, but it sure as hell wasn't *helping* you."

"I never said it was."

"No," he agreed. "That's where I blew it. It was top on my mind and out it came."

Her anger eased just a bit. "Top on your mind?"

"Damn, it was good, Sharon. Dangerous, but good. I don't want you getting hurt because I can't control my lust for you. Looks like we got to the hurting part, anyway."

His lust for her? A shiver of pure sensuality rippled through her, dampening her anger even more. No! She fought it down. No more of that. Lust was just lust. About that much he was right.

"What happened?" he asked. "I get the feeling that

us having such a good time together opened wounds. I never want to do that to you."

Her lips felt stiff as she answered, forcing herself to be uncomfortably truthful. "Sometimes wounds are festering under the scar tissue. Lancing them is good. That's what happened."

"Because we...?" He didn't finish the question.

"Yes, in part. I felt alive again. I realized I wanted to live again, and enjoy everything again, and then I got to thinking about all I'd missed. It all just backed up like a sewer."

Several heartbeats later, he spoke. "I guess that's good?"

"I don't know. It sure hurt. But I need to face it and sort it out."

"I get that," he said after a moment. "Facing things can be tough. I guess I should leave you alone. I just wanted you to know I didn't mean to be insulting. It was special to me. I just didn't think it was helpful."

"Maybe it was, for me."

"Okay." He paused, then started to turn away, but she stopped him.

"Did it help you at all, Liam?"

He hesitated. "Not really. Not if by help you mean something good, but I guess you don't since it managed to rip you wide-open. I guess that's something we should avoid."

He was going off on his own tangent again. Part of her said to let him go, but part of her refused to let it drop here. Maybe she was naive enough to need to believe it hadn't simply been mechanics and biology for either of them.

"Something bad happened to you after we were together?" she asked quietly.

"Not exactly." He sighed. "It's hard to say. I guess I felt lonely later. I never had what you and Chet had. I always figured it would come someday, but…well, I just never had it. And now it looks like it'll probably never happen."

"Why not?"

"Look at me, Sharon. Look at the million little things you do for me to keep me going through a day. I'm broken, damn it. Yeah, I keep finding out I can deal with some things. I can paint a barn. I can follow decent directions if I can sort through them. You're helping me to read. But there's no telling how many more ways I'm broken that I don't even know yet. I guess I'm going to find out. Who's gonna want to put up with that and my moods? What if I lose it and go ballistic? I can't even promise not to do that. Push me hard enough, and I probably will."

"Go ballistic how?"

"Rant, throw things, smash things. You think any woman wants to live with that kind of time bomb? Or even consider having kids in that situation? I'm not sure that I've got a tight tether on myself."

"Well," she said slowly, "you didn't kill those guys in the parking lot."

"Because that guy stepped in."

"Have you considered that even though he stepped in, you could have still acted out?"

He didn't answer.

"You didn't have to stop just because one guy spoke up for you."

He just shook his head. "You don't know how many

times a day I just want to smash something. It's not as often here. I don't feel pushed by much, but I still feel it. And I get so damn mad at myself."

Then he shook his head again. "I came up here to talk about you, not about me."

"Right now it seems to be the same subject. I wonder if that hot chocolate is cold."

"Probably."

"Then I'll heat it up. Let's go downstairs." She drew him out of her room, away from the bed she had shared with Chet that suddenly seemed too damn inviting. Look at the two of them, she thought to herself. They were likely to use each other as a bandage if they weren't careful.

The kitchen seemed ever so much safer, although considering what had happened on the counter only a few hours ago, that was open to question.

She poured the cocoa back into the pan and put it on simmer, stirring gently so a skin didn't form. She listened to him pace behind her, but eventually he settled on a chair.

She refilled the mugs and returned with them to the table. "We're a mess," she announced.

"You're not that much of a mess," he argued.

"That's debatable. When you walked up that driveway I was just trying to shake myself out of the paralysis I've been dealing with since Chet passed. Everything around here was going to hell, and I knew I needed to do something about it, but I couldn't make myself. Then you came, and things around here are getting fixed."

"What little I can do."

"Stop knocking yourself. And for God's sake, don't hate yourself because you were wounded. I can understand being frustrated and angry, but there's no reason on earth to hate yourself for it. It's beyond your control."

"But I remember," he said tautly. "I remember how I *used* to be. That's part of what's so frustrating, being able to remember what I used to be able to do, and not being able to do it now."

"I know." She sighed. "I know. Lots of people have to face that, and it stinks. I had a student in one of my classes who was paralyzed in a fall. When he came back to school, he was angry as hell. I couldn't blame him for that at all. Real people aren't Tiny Tims."

He furrowed his brow. "You mean from *A Christmas Carol?*"

"Yeah, that kid. Anyway, real people have to get over a whole bunch of stuff when something bad like this happens. Anger is part of it."

"It's grief, they told me."

"It probably is, but it's probably a whole lot more, too."

"I don't know."

"I don't, either," she admitted. "I'm not an expert. Look at me. I've had almost a year and a half to get used to losing Chet, and I'm still coming out of some kind of fog. I was even having a temper tantrum out there earlier tonight. I've never done that before."

"You've never had a tantrum?"

"Not that kind, not since I was little. But there I was, beating my fists on the ground." One corner of her mouth lifted. "It helped. So if you feel a need…"

"I'll try to beat on the ground, not the walls." He shifted, then drank some cocoa.

She waited, giving them both some space. All in all it had been a pretty intense evening. She visited places she hadn't even imagined existed inside of her. Feeling cheated, not just by Chet's death, but by their whole marriage. Such a thought had never crossed her mind before.

He spoke. "There's a kind of unspoken practice in combat. After you've lost a couple of buddies, you decide not to make any new ones. Not really. You develop a shell and don't let the new guys get close."

She nodded.

"You were doing that, weren't you?"

"I guess so. Exactly that."

"Well, I have been, too. I let you get close. I'm not sure that's a good thing."

Then he rose and walked out the back door.

Here we go again, Sharon thought. She stared down into her mug. He had even more reason than she to keep that carapace over his heart. His losses were a whole lot bigger.

After all, he'd lost Chet, too, and they'd been buddies for over twelve years. Even she couldn't claim that. Had he grieved? Of course he had. He probably still did.

Then there were his cognitive deficits, truly hard to deal with, something that could jump up and bite him at any time. He had a plate far fuller than her own.

From what he had said, she gathered that their sex earlier had wakened longings in him, too, longings for the kind of life he'd once imagined would be his, but now felt he was denied forever.

That was even worse than what she was feeling. She had to deal with the past while having the future wide-open to her. He felt his future was narrowed, possibly completely, because nobody would want to put up with him.

She considered those outbursts, although she hadn't seen one, only seen the effects when he strode away, and wondered if he could even hold a real job if he needed to walk away when the pressure got to be too much. Maybe not.

Although he was doing just fine here. As far as she was concerned, he could stay forever if he wanted.

Then a shock ripped through her. He was going to leave. Soon. He'd just said he shouldn't have let her get so close.

Oh, God! All of a sudden she wondered if she could bear that.

She jumped up and ran to the door, stepping out onto the small back porch. Even with the brilliance of the frosty moonlight, she couldn't see him anywhere. No sign of a shadow striding across open fields. The barn, perhaps?

But just as she started to take a step, she stopped herself. He needed space. She couldn't deprive him of that.

But, God, he'd better come back, because she didn't know how she would handle it if he didn't.

She was in deep trouble, she realized. Returning inside, she sat at the table and waited. It was going to be a hell of a long night.

Chapter Ten

Summer dawns came early in these parts. The eastern sky had turned fiery red by the time Liam returned to the house. Sharon had sagged over her mug, having switched to coffee from hot chocolate hours ago. She turned as he entered the door, her face haggard, her eyes rimmed purple with fatigue.

"You didn't stay up all night?" He sounded shocked.

"I was worried," she admitted.

"I've been in far more dangerous places than your grazing land."

She didn't even smile. "I'm sure."

"You need to sleep."

"I will. Later."

So he grabbed a coffee and sat at the table with her. "When's that paint coming for the barn?"

"Maybe today. Impatient?"

"I need the hard work."

She nodded, then looked down at the table again.

"Does that red sky mean rain today?"

She shrugged. "Probably not. That old sailor's saw doesn't work well here. Unless we're overcast."

"Didn't see any."

She didn't say any more. The questions foremost on her mind had to do with what he had been thinking about while he strode through the night. She knew what she'd been thinking about, and a lot of it was scary.

"You weren't really worried about me."

At his statement she looked at him, feeling a tired irritation. "Oh, really? I stay up all night when I'm feeling great?"

"Then why don't you talk to me about it?"

"Why don't you tell me what set you running off into the night? What worries *you?*"

They exchanged stares, then the quiet extended, an enveloping blanket of tension. Finally, Sharon could take it no more. "You're such a damn sphinx. You talk about some things, but not really about how you're feeling about anything. It's like you analyze yourself internally and leave me wondering all the time. Whatever leashes they told you to put on yourself have turned into a cage, Liam."

"Maybe for good reason."

"Maybe. How would I know? All I know for the most part is what I see of you. Not what you think about anything. Not what you feel about anything."

"Why do you need to know all that stuff?"

She bit her lip, feeling again the ache he aroused in her all too easily, the yearning for things she didn't dare name. It wasn't just sex anymore, and that scared her. "Because I care," she admitted quietly.

He swore. "Is that wise? Well, hell, I care about you, too, but I still have to ask if that's wise. I can guarantee there's no future I can offer you."

"Why? Because you're broken?"

"Because I haven't even figured out who I am yet. The new and not-so-improved version of me, anyway."

"I think you have the same values you used to."

"God, I hope so. But in the past I never would have just blurted out that I wanted in a woman."

"What's so bad about that?" she demanded. "Is it better to conceal it in subterfuge?"

"Subterfuge?"

"Yeah, dinners out, long walks holding hands, flowers and candy. Isn't that where it always starts? Why not just be honest?"

"Because that's not the kind of thing a guy is supposed to say. Not out of the blue like that. If that doesn't give you an indication of what's wrong with me..."

"I'm tired of hearing what's wrong with you. How about what's right with you?"

He looked flummoxed.

"See?" she said. "They filled your head with all these warnings about everything that's wrong with Liam. Well, I don't see a whole lot that's wrong with you. Yeah, you're moody. So? You can't read much. So? You can sure paint a barn. You can even straighten one up. I bet if I got a damn goat you'd learn every bit as fast as me how to take care of it."

"If I didn't forget."

"I might forget a few things until they become habit."

He just stared at her with something like amazement. "You haven't seen it all."

"I haven't seen you smash anything. I've sure watched you stomp off by yourself often enough. What else?"

"I have freaking nightmares. Sometimes I don't exactly remember where I'm at."

"Flashbacks?"

"Sometimes. Sometimes I just can't remember where I am in time or space. That's real useful. It's part of the reason I need to stay busy. If I've got something in my hand, if I'm talking to myself, I've got an anchor. That would make anyone crazy to put up with for long."

"It's not bothering me."

"So what are you saying?"

"What I've said before. Start thinking of the good things about who you are now. For heaven's sake, you hiked across the country to deliver a letter, and now you're helping me out with things I could never have done otherwise."

"Even when you have to help me?"

"The odd thing is, I don't mind. It makes me feel useful, too. I'm not just standing around watching some man fix my property. I'm helping, too."

He stared at her. Evidently he wasn't buying that it was that simple. "And what about you?" he asked.

"What about me?"

"What are you looking for? Just getting the place fixed up?"

That hurt. It hurt so much that she had to look away and swallow a few times. That wasn't it at all, but she couldn't explain the reasons she wanted Liam to stay because she didn't fully know why herself. Had she just been lonely too long? Or was it something more? She feared the latter. That way lay the worst pain of all.

"I don't know," she said finally. "I just know I like you being here."

"That's what worries me," he said quietly. "That we'll get to like this setup for all the wrong reasons."

She couldn't deny it concerned her, too. But she'd been thinking long and hard during the night as she waited for him to return. "Maybe we should just stop worrying long-term and just take everything a day at a time. Unless you're in a rush to get away."

"Getting away from you is the last thing I want right now," he said frankly.

"Good. Then stick around. I'm going to nap on the couch until Ed arrives with the paint. He's bringing the sprayer if you want to save some labor."

He shook his head. "Like I said, I'd rather do it the hard way. I'm missing the gym."

"Okay." Smiling faintly, she rose, but as she started to pass him, he caught her hand. Then, astonishing her, he raised it and pressed a kiss to the back of it. "You're a special lady," he said huskily.

After the miserable night, her heart felt incredibly light as she headed for the sofa.

He needed sleep as much as Sharon did, but he was still too wound up. Liam sat at the table, not yet worn out enough from his long walk, hoping the paint would arrive so he would get started on the barn.

He clenched and unclenched his fists, trying to ease the tension that crackled along his nerves. What the hell was he getting into here? Could he even judge?

Sharon was right about one thing: he'd been cut loose

after a whole heap of warnings about his new limitations, followed by a cheery, "But you should improve with time. You've improved a lot already."

What did that mean? How long would it take? How would he know when he was improving? And whatever improvements might be happening, he still had the temper and frustration to deal with. The nightmares. The losing himself in time, the forgetting what he was doing unless he talked himself through it or had some physical reminder to pull him back.

Why would anyone want to deal with all that? But Sharon didn't mind, and that suddenly seemed like absolutely the scariest thing of all.

Someone who didn't mind his outbursts, his explosive moods that he could handle only by walking them off. Sometimes the rest of it didn't seem so bad, not even the nightmares, or the occasional flashback. What drove him nuts was being unable to follow a line start to finish without losing track of where he was without some reminder.

That drove him crazy.

Sharon was beginning to drive him crazy, too. The thing was, with her it wasn't a bad crazy. It was a good crazy, and that really worried him.

Brain damage or not, he hadn't completely forgotten how to gauge other people, how to be concerned about them, too. She was getting attached. So was he. And that could turn out to be so bad if it was for the wrong reasons on either side.

He'd found a haven here. That wasn't necessarily a good thing if he clung to it simply because he could handle things better here. Low pressure, a nice lady to whom he was attracted… Yeah, that could be a bad thing. Because that was not a good reason to trash someone else by grabbing for a lifeline that might only be temporary.

How could he tell what he was reaching for here? He didn't know. And the last thing on earth he wanted was to bring more grief to Chet's widow.

But he wanted her. The more he was with her, the deeper the craving seemed to grow. He sure hadn't felt that for any of the women at the rehab place, and there'd been plenty of pretty ones. No, he wanted Sharon, and he was beginning to think that walking away would rip him up good.

But thinking about himself was selfish. He needed to think about her.

Unfortunately, thinking about her only brought him around full circle. He liked her, yes. He wanted her, yes. But that wasn't enough, especially when he looked down the tunnel of his future and couldn't figure out what should be there. He owed any woman more than that, more than a half-reborn man.

But maybe he was making a mountain out of a molehill. He didn't know what Sharon was feeling or wanting. Hell, she was probably as wary as he was.

That made him feel a little better, but he made up his mind to one thing: he was going to have to leave as soon as he was through painting the barn. They both needed time and space from a situation that was getting too cozy too easily.

Yeah, he'd finish the barn and resume his trek to nowhere. Maybe when he'd been gone a month or so, they'd have clearer heads. Maybe he'd discover, like she said, that he wasn't as badly messed up as he thought.

But dang, he'd have liked to help her with those

goats. He'd have liked to help her build that dream she and Chet had shared.

He'd have liked a lot of things. Life wasn't often kind enough to listen.

Sharon woke to a gentle voice calling her, and when she opened drowsy eyes, she saw Liam bent over her. Her heart leapt at the sight, and she drank in the lines of his face, the strength of his build, and realized she would have preferred to be wakened by his touches, by his lovemaking.

The sleepy wish lasted only a second or two before shock zapped through her and she sat bolt upright. They were dangerous feelings for a man she believed had every intention of moving on. Hadn't he told her he couldn't offer her a future?

She'd be a fool not to listen.

"Ed's here," he said.

"Thanks." She popped up off the couch feeling royally grungy, and that didn't even include the sharp sand in her eyes. It'd been a long night, caused by her own foolishness, she thought wearily. She needn't have sat up waiting for Liam. He could take care of himself, she was sure.

But in her heart of hearts she knew that wasn't why she'd stayed up. She'd feared he wouldn't come back. Great. Super. She felt as if her emotions had taken a roller-coaster ride without her permission.

Liam stepped back, giving her plenty of space to rise. So the guy who had kissed her hand a couple of hours ago was now afraid to brush against her. Great. Just great.

Irritable, yet feeling a horrible sense of impending

loss, she went outside to greet Ed. He looked chipper and alert, which only made her feel grumpier. She could feel Liam standing on the porch as she went down to greet Ed, have him put the paint in the barn and sign the slip for it.

"So how's your friend working out?" Ed asked.

"Great," she said. "Don't leave the sprayer, though."

"C'mon, it'll make the job easier. I can't believe he painted that whole damn building by hand."

"I like the work."

The unexpectedness of Liam's voice so nearby almost made Sharon jump. She had thought he was still back on the porch.

"Suit yourself," Ed said with a shrug. "Anything else?"

"Not for now," answered Sharon with faked cheer. "I know where to find you if we need more supplies."

"That you do. Three days before the next delivery?"

"Thanks."

He waved as he drove away, leaving her and Liam standing in the yard before the barn where the cans of paint sat in a neat row.

"I'll start now," Liam said.

"Like hell you will. You haven't had any more sleep than I have and if you take a fall, I'll have to call the air rescue. We need sleep and something to eat."

Without looking at him, she marched toward the house. A few seconds later she sensed him following her.

Whatever resolutions they'd both been making died as she climbed the steps. Weary as she was, she stumbled. He caught her.

Everything went out of control in an instant. His

arms around her felt so damn good, and the desire she felt for him surged like a forceful fountain. God, she wanted this man. Wanted him. Reason couldn't beat that down.

As soon as he caught her against his hard body, she looked up and saw the same fire in his gaze. He wanted her, just like he'd said, and the sight of his hunger, printed so clearly on his face, fueled hers like tinder in a fire.

Their eyes locked for one breathless instant. Then, without a word, he picked her up, eased her through the screen door, and headed up the stairs. This was going to be no kitchen-counter quickie. Her insides clenched with sheer passion.

She looped her arms around his neck, surrendering already, beyond caring about all the roadblocks she had tried to throw up. Whatever it cost, she was going to steal these moments from life, and she was damned if she would ever regret them.

At the top of the stairs he didn't even hesitate. He carried her to the room he was using, thank goodness. The double bed in there would be ample and there was a line she wasn't ready to cross in her own bed.

But the thought barely crossed her mind. More important things were building, like the rumblings just before a summer storm.

He said only one thing as he let her slide to her feet. "You won't hate me?"

"Never."

He searched her face briefly, then swooped in for a kiss. Nothing gentle and nothing sweet happened then. What had been suppressed for too long took charge. She pulled at his clothes. He pulled at hers.

The room filled with the sound of their heavy breathing, the sound of buttons and snaps popping. Clothes flew every which way, but Sharon was hardly aware of anything but the drive to be naked with him, to tumble onto the bed.

Then, suddenly it seemed, they were both nude.

"Let me look at you," he said huskily.

For an instant, she nearly froze with embarrassment as he stepped back, but when she saw the look on his face, her shyness fled.

"Damn, you're gorgeous."

"So are you," she said as she trailed her eyes over him. A fine physique, a little overdeveloped from all that working out, but fine nonetheless. And scars. She almost gasped as she saw them, but swallowed the sound. More than anything she feared she might drive him away. Not now. No way.

But the marks were there. The head injury might be invisible, but not the other wounds. He'd been shot. She hadn't known that. He had slashing scars here and there, but she couldn't guess what from. She'd ask later. Much later. Right now nothing could be allowed to come between them.

He paused long enough to pull out a condom and roll it on, then smiled almost sleepily at her.

"Turn for me?" he asked.

Feeling more confident now, she turned slowly for him, heard the sigh escape him. "You're perfect."

She didn't think so, but all that mattered was what he thought. As she faced him again, she couldn't resist cupping her own breasts as if offering them to him.

He groaned and reached for her instantly, carrying her down onto the bed with him.

There was absolutely no feeling on Earth like skin on skin. Nothing like legs tangling, arms wrapping, mouths meeting. Nothing like moans and sighs answered as the journey began.

Hearing him groan her name lifted her even higher. But even with their experience yesterday, the moment felt filled with hungry desperation. There was little finesse between them, just a passionate meeting and melding. Without warning, he lifted her to straddle him as he lay on his back. She didn't hesitate. Reaching for his hardened staff, she took him into her, settling on him until he filled her completely, feeling that wonderful sense of stretching and fullness she hadn't felt in so long. She threw her head back, savoring the exquisite sensation of intimate connection.

Then he gripped her arms and tugged. "Ride me," he demanded.

She was only too happy to do it. Leaning forward until she was propped on her hands, she slid forward and back, felt him fill her again and again. The throbbing deep within her strengthened rapidly until it was so hard she ached with each new pulse.

His hands found her breasts, amplifying her pleasure as he kneaded her, brushing his thumbs over her nipples, drawing shudders and moans from her.

So fast, too fast, she was reaching the peak. Then he grabbed her naked hips, forcing her rhythm, carrying her to the highest peak so rapidly she felt she couldn't catch her breath.

An instant later, she shattered in an orgasm so intense it tore a cry from her. As she started to sag, she felt him buck once more, then felt the unmistakable pulsation of his staff as he jetted into her.

An instant later she collapsed and was surrounded by his arms. Everything else vanished, except the slowly weakening throbbing in her body. And with each of those quieting throbs, a shiver passed through her.

She felt sated. Truly sated.

He rolled her off him gently. "Be right back," he murmured, dropping a kiss on her lips.

She tried to hang on to his hand. A quiet chuckle escaped him. "There's more, darlin'. Much more."

Hazy, not quite drowsy, she lay on the coverlet while her body told her she was ready for more. Much more. All of it. All night, all day, never-ending more of Liam. It had been wild, basic, fast. She had never done that before, and it kind of amazed her that she had returned to elemental feeling so fast.

But she smiled into the empty room as she recalled the hot and ready way they had coupled. Basic, but perfect.

And he'd called her "darlin'." She liked it. Nobody had ever called her that before. Not once. That was another special thing about Liam.

Before reality could intrude on the glow, he returned, tugged some more condoms out of his pack and threw them on the bedside table. She smiled again as she saw them.

Then he stretched out beside her, his head propped on his hand, and smiled at her.

"Gorgeous," he said again.

As his gaze swept over her, she felt it like a physical touch. Nerve endings sizzled as if he had brushed his hands over her.

She looked him over, too, admiring him, and finally

reached out to touch him, savoring the feel of his skin beneath her palms and fingers. She didn't ask about the scars. None of that was going to shatter this precious feeling.

He sighed as she touched him, closing his eyes briefly before reaching out to reciprocate. His hand passed slowly over her every curve, as if he were memorizing her contours.

"Exquisite," he murmured.

"So are you."

He didn't argue. For once he didn't argue when she said something nice about him. That seemed like a total triumph to her, and as energy began to return to her limbs, she wanted him again. Now. Fast and furious.

But he didn't seem in the mood for that. He took his time fondling her, awakening her again. First he explored her breasts, cupping their weight, giving a shuddering sigh as her nipples hardened. Then he bent his mouth to her, sucking at first gently on each nipple. When he lifted his head she felt the coolness of the air on the dampness, and it added to the building pleasure in her.

She didn't want to push him, though. Men didn't get ready again as soon as women did. She had read that.

But he didn't seem to care. He ministered to her breasts until she felt herself spiraling upward again into passion. Just that and no more, yet she felt as if she were climbing that incredible mountain again, the summit coming closer with each pull of his mouth on her breasts.

When her hips finally rolled in response, he gave a quiet chuckle. A moment later, he rolled onto her, settling himself between her legs and making her feel so very open and vulnerable. Another shiver of delight passed through her as he smiled down at her.

"You're one sexy woman." His voice was low and husky.

He took her breast into his mouth again, this time nipping at her nipple and drawing a little cry from her.

"Definitely sexy."

Then, little by little he trailed his mouth downward, causing renewed shivers as he sprinkled kissed over her abdomen. Every part of her became so alive to his caresses that she felt like a bundle of total sensuality.

Instinctively she reached for his shoulders as he slid even lower. Her legs lifted, trying to wrap around him, her whole body needing to be as open as possible to him.

But he continued her torment, his hands reaching up to find her breasts as he continued to kiss and lick her belly. Her hips rocked upward again, needing deeper touches, deeper pressures, which he withheld. With each touch of his hands and mouth, she felt an opening deep inside her, a welcoming need for this man and everything he could both give and take from her.

She felt like a rose blooming in a rare desert rain. Opening, opening...

She wanted him in her again. Now. But he still withheld as he continued to quest with hands and mouth for every sensitive part of her. She couldn't force him closer; he just kept on teasing her until she thought she would go out of her mind.

Finally she cried out his name. "Liam!"

For one heart-stopping instant everything halted. Then she felt him slide lower and wonder of wonders his fingers touched her petals, stroking them, parting them. A violent shudder of delight ripped through her and a long moan escaped her.

Oh, please, please...

Held in thrall by the passion he awoke so easily in her, she didn't know if she begged out loud or only deep inside. Again and again his fingers brushed her so lightly it was maddening and thrilling all at once.

Her hips responded insistently, out of control. There was no control left in her, only hunger. "Please..." The sigh escaped her.

His hot, wet mouth found her most vulnerable place, the first lash of his tongue painful in its intensity. Another cry escaped her and she almost jerked away, but his hands gripped her hips, holding her. He seemed to be drinking from her, alternately sucking and licking that most sensitive nub. Each sensation fueled the conflagration he had unleashed in her. Aflame with desire, she felt as if she were riding a shooting star.

Completion came, so aching and deep it filled her entire body. Just as she was ready to sink back to Earth, his mouth went to work again, feeding the quieting throbbing until it was no longer quieting, but growing strong yet again. She couldn't...she couldn't...

But she did. With a powerful intensity she knew she would never forget, he brought her an orgasm that shattered her very being into a thousand flaming pieces.

At the final moment, she was helpless to do anything but cry his name.

Liam lay with his cheek on her belly, listening to the thunder of her pulse gradually subside as he tried to both hold her and shield her.

A kind of peace flowed through him, easing him in a way he hadn't felt eased in a long time. He may have just made a huge mistake for both of them, but it was hard to care when he was feeling so good.

He had given Sharon a precious gift, something he had rarely ever wanted to give a woman. He could feel that gift pulsing through her, feel it in the limpness of her body, hear it in her ragged breathing.

Apparently, he wasn't messed up that way, and it felt damn good. He could paint Sharon's barn and house, and he could give her some great sex. It didn't make him special or important, but it made him feel like a man again. All the other problems he'd been living with felt minuscule by comparison.

Damn, she was fantastic. Open and eager to whatever he offered, giving herself without reservation. How often did you find that? Not very.

Don't toy with her.

Was that what he had just done? God, he hoped not. But it had been building between them. He saw it in her glances, sometimes written on her face, and he knew they were both trying to ignore it. Trying not to give in. Now they had given in, and by his estimation, whatever the price, this was going to stay with him as a wondrous time he would never regret. Never.

He could have stayed like this forever.

It wouldn't be enough, though. His chest ached as he thought about it, knowing that you couldn't build a life on a fairy-tale experience. She needed a whole man, not a messed up one who would only make her life harder.

He'd deal with that later. He just knew he'd been wanting her almost since the first instant he clapped eyes on her. Wanting her in a way that simply wouldn't subside or be ignored.

She had said she wanted him, too. And like some kind of idiot, he had thought that quickie yesterday would put it to rest for both of them. Needs satisfied, they could go on without the constant yearning.

How wrong he'd been. His taste for her had simply grown even bigger, and apparently hers had, too.

Damn, he wanted to cling to her right now and pretend tomorrow would never come. But it always came. Good or bad, it always came. Reality would return.

But for right now, he could banish it.

"Liam?"

She breathed his name. Hearing it, he lifted his head.

"Hold me," she said huskily.

So he slid up over her, turned on his side and drew her into his arms, throwing one leg over hers.

"That was fantastic," she whispered.

"It sure was."

"I didn't know I could…could…"

Damn, she was blushing. "Never before?" he asked, absolutely delighted. He was sure a sappy grin creased his face.

"I thought only other women could do that…"

"Wow." That amazed him. Of course, he could understand why she might not know. He was feeling sleepy enough for two men right now. It would have been easy to doze off right after their first round, and only a desire to please her had kept him going.

She tipped her head and kissed his cheek. Then she giggled. "You smell like me."

"Can't imagine why."

That unleashed another giggle.

"Want me to go wash?"

"Don't you dare move." She burrowed closer into his embrace until her head rested on his shoulder. Her arm wound around his waist. "You can add this to the list of things that make you wonderful."

He liked the sound of that a whole lot. "It's not much…"

She reached up to lay a finger over his lips. "We're not going to do that. Not now. How are you?"

"Frankly? I'm happy. I can't ever remember feeling this happy."

"That's a sweet thing to say."

"A true one." Which was probably a sad comment on his entire life, but definitely true. He gave her a gentle squeeze.

"I feel weak as a kitten," she remarked.

"Then sleep."

"I don't want to sleep. I don't want to waste a minute with you."

Alarm bells clanged, but his current contentment muted them. He had a lot of experience living in the moment. Combat had taught that lesson quickly. Tomorrow would come or it wouldn't. In this case it probably would since he didn't expect any incoming rounds, but tomorrow was soon enough to deal with any fallout from this.

He certainly wasn't going to waste right now on things that hadn't happened yet, that might not happen. Just take the good that life offered because you never knew when it might offer something good again.

It had been a long, sleepless night for both of them. He barely realized that he was falling asleep before it carried him away.

* * *

Sharon lay awake a little longer, watching him sleep, feeling the growing need for some sleep herself, but she fought it off as long as she could. He had shown her a piece of heaven, and she wanted to replay every single instant in her mind repeatedly, as if to engrave it so that not a single moment would ever be forgotten.

But she was exhausted from the long night, and pleasantly so from their lovemaking, and no matter how hard she fought it off, sleep claimed her. She slipped into wonderful dreams of golden fields, blue sky and sunshine.

"Liam!"

The sharp cry woke him from a dark nightmare to a late golden afternoon. He sat up instantly, alert, ready for anything.

"Liam!"

It was hard, but he yanked himself out of that dark place into the present to see a naked Sharon kneeling beside him, looking at him with concern.

"You were having a terrible nightmare," she said. "Are you all right?"

"No." He closed his eyes, then reopened them. He stumbled out of the bed and began grabbing his clothes.

"Liam?"

"Damn it, Sharon, I held Chet in my arms while he died!"

He jammed his feet into socks and boots and headed for the door.

"Don't run away from this. Don't you dare!"

He just kept going.

* * *

Sharon struggled into her clothes, her fingers misbehaving on every button. He'd held Chet while he died. God! But he better not head for the hills, not now. They had to deal with this. Both of them.

Feeling shaky, she stumbled downstairs at last, afraid she would see no sign of him. She about panicked when he wasn't in the kitchen or living room, but then she saw him standing out on the front porch. At least he hadn't taken off.

The screen door creaked as she stepped outside. She said nothing, but simply went to stand beside him. When the silence had stretched forever, and the sun had disappeared behind the nearby mountains, a chill crept into the air.

She was losing him. Somehow she had to draw him back. Somehow.

"You said it was instantaneous." She hated the almost accusatory tone, but it made him stir. Until that moment he had been as still as stone.

"It was, for him. He never woke up. It was longer for me."

"Oh, God." Her hand flew to her mouth, and she bit her knuckle.

"I tried to save him. I tried, I swear. But nothing was working, and when our medic reached us, he tried, too. Nothing worked. So finally I just held him. Nobody wants to die alone."

She couldn't stop the sob that ripped its way out of her, or the tears that began to pour. Liam seemed to shake himself, then turned and wrapped her tightly in his arms.

"I'm sorry I couldn't save him. I'm sorry you had to hear that. I'm so sorry, Sharon."

"I'm sorry for you," she said between sobs. "Sorry you had to endure that. I'm glad you were there for him, though."

"I was. I swear I was."

She absolutely believed him. But when she stacked his loss against hers, they both looked pretty much the same: huge, enormous. Enough to steal the light and warmth from the day.

"Then don't apologize to me," she gasped. "Please. I'm so glad he wasn't alone, I can't tell you."

She wrapped her arms around his waist and thought, really thought, about his losses. Not only his brain injury, but the loss of his old life, and his best friend and God knew how many other friends. He had suffered too much. More than anyone should have to.

Yet he was still here and she thanked God for it. "I'm glad you're here," she said, then hiccuped. "I'm so glad you're here."

He was strong in ways she hoped she never had to learn to be strong. She wished he could see it.

Leaning back a little within the circle of his arms, she reached up and cupped his face. His eyes, which had been closed, opened at that, and in those light green orbs she saw a measure of the anguish that tormented him.

"You're a good and strong man," she said firmly. "I am so glad you're here with me."

He shook his head a little, as if denying it. She wondered if anyone or anything would ever convince him that he wasn't broken in the ways that mattered.

And she might never know. Chet's death had just thrust itself between them again. She could only wonder if he was feeling guilty for their lovemaking, feeling he had betrayed Chet. She didn't know how to bring it up.

What she did know was that she didn't feel that way at all. A little while ago, her heart had been singing with happiness. Every human was entitled to happiness.

"Come inside," she begged. "Let's make coffee and something to eat. If you want to talk, we'll talk. If not, we'll just be together."

He looked past her. "I was going to start painting."

Withdrawal. She felt it and her heart squeezed. "It's too late in the day. The light is awful now. Please, come inside with me."

The last of the stiffness slowly seeped out of him. Finally, he reached up to cover one of her hands with his. "Okay," he said.

But she felt he had gone to a planet a billion miles away.

Inside she started a fresh pot of coffee, then pulled some cold cuts from the fridge and began to make ham sandwiches. Somehow, she thought, they had to edge back from this precipice. She felt as if everything were hanging in the balance of whatever might come next.

"Lettuce?" she asked. "Mayo? Mustard?"

"Whatever."

Oh, she didn't like the sound of that. A feeling of desperation began to grow in her. Even if they had no future, she still wasn't ready to lose him. No way. Friends for life would be better by far than Liam picking up his backpack and walking away for good.

She put the sandwiches on the table. Then an impulse came to her. Picking up the phone, she dialed Ransom Laird. "Ransom? I'm looking for a goat or two to try my hand. Dr. Windwalker said you were the man…Yes. Okay, tomorrow morning. Thanks."

Then she sat at the table and waited for a response. A few more minutes passed, then Liam picked up his sandwich and took a large bite.

"I go to these places sometimes," he offered finally. "They're not pretty."

"The war?"

"The wars. Yeah. It's usually in nightmares, which is better than having it happen while I'm awake."

"I'm sorry."

"Me, too. But there it is. I just have to deal."

Ignoring her own sandwich, she tried to think of one useful thing to say. She couldn't.

"Sorry if I scared you."

She shook her head. "You didn't scare me. I was worried about you. That's very different."

He didn't reply. She got up and poured the coffee for them. She had a feeling it was going to be another long night.

Then he seemed to shake himself. "You decided about the goats?"

"Yes. And I'd like you to be here because I may need your help."

Then he said something that made her feel worlds better. "I wasn't planning on being anywhere else."

"You're sure? Because a little while ago I got the feeling you were going to take off."

"I thought about it." No explanations, no apology. Statement of fact.

"What changed your mind?"

"You can either run or you can stand your ground. It's time to stand my ground. If you can stand me."

"I'm horrified that you'd even ask." Not after what they had shared. But then he'd dreamed of Chet. Maybe she wasn't good for him.

She gnawed her lip, then lifted her sandwich, figuring she'd do herself more good by gnawing on some ham and bread.

"Maybe," she said eventually, "being with me isn't good for you."

"Don't even say that!" Finally some animation in his face. "Don't think it. No, I've got some messes of my own to deal with, and they don't have anything to do with you."

"I brought back memories of Chet."

"I never forget Chet, probably any more than you do. No, that wasn't anything new. He was my brother. I mean that. More than a friend. I loved him, Sharon. The way I'd have loved a brother. Different from what you felt, but just as strong."

"Yes." She waited, then took another bite. He resumed eating, punctuating it with sips of coffee. She wondered where this was going, or if it was going anywhere at all.

But at least he didn't seem so withdrawn.

He finished both his sandwiches then went to get the coffeepot and refill their mugs. She still hadn't made it through half of hers.

"Sorry I upset you," he said. "I'll probably do that from time to time."

"I can live with it."

"We'll see," he said.

She wondered what he meant by that. *We'll see.* So leaving was still on his list. Either that or he believed she would tire of him.

It occurred to her that she owed herself and him some very serious thinking. No more back-and-forthing, but a decision. Did she want Liam around long-term? Even as just a friend? Could she deal with this?

Although dealing didn't seem to be her problem. Sometimes she got upset when he disappeared to manage his frustration and anger. Sometimes she just let it go. And sometimes she just felt lonely. She could handle that. His deficits? She probably didn't know all of them yet, but from what she had seen they wouldn't exactly make huge ripples around here, especially as he grew less frustrated.

The way he sometimes just clammed up? But he was doing less of that. He'd just told her about Chet, which must have been painful for him, especially since he knew it would pain her. If there was one thing she'd learned about Liam, for all he'd been a soldier, in many ways he was a gentle soul. Chet had had harder edges when he came home, maybe because he really never had a lot of time to wind down before he had to start winding up again. It wasn't that he'd been cruel. By no means. But there was a gentleness to Liam at times that surprised her.

But mostly she had to be sure, because the last thing on Earth she wanted to do was wound Liam again. She had to know her own mind, even though the possibility would always remain that he would one day walk away.

She had to know what she wanted, what her limits were, and then make them clear so that he knew where she stood. So he could make a decision himself about whether he needed to move on.

God, she hated the thought of him leaving, but if that

was what would be best for one or both of them, then she was going to have to face up to it.

And it was going to be difficult to be so hardheaded when her emotions were running so strongly. But she had to do it.

"So you've decided to do that goat thing?" he asked again as they were cleaning up, as if he felt the need to break the silence and had seized the first thing he thought of.

"I'm just talking to Ransom about it. That okay with you?"

"I don't have a right to say anything about it."

She turned to face him, sponge in hand. "You have a right. You're going to be helping me. You've never said much about what you think about it."

"I like the idea." He hesitated. "Sharon, think about it, please. If I stay, I'm going to be a hanger-on, basically. I don't think I could hold a job, at least not yet. I get a disability check and have plenty of savings, and I could help out that way, but do you really want a dependent?"

The question nearly floored her. "Is that how you feel? Am I making you feel that way?"

He hesitated. "No. I'm just feeling that way."

"So how do you count what you've been doing around here?"

"Just helping."

"Has it occurred to you that except for your help I'd need to hire someone? As it is, I'd have to provide room and board plus pay to anyone else. Heck, I wouldn't want a stranger living in this house with me, so I'd have to pay a whole lot for a handyman. In fact, I ought to be paying you something."

He shook his head. She dropped the sponge and stared at him, giving him space to react to what she had said.

"It wouldn't be right," he said finally, "for me to continue taking from you. You can't possibly be making that much as a teacher. You're probably mostly scraping by with a place like this. I need to contribute if I'm going to stay."

"You *are* contributing."

His expression became slightly mulish, a stubbornness she hadn't seen in him before. "Not enough. Not by my standards."

At first she struggled with a sense of offense, because he felt she needed more from him. As if. Did he really think that barn had gotten into that shape because she could paint and clean it by herself? Or the house?

But then she realized something more essential about him. This was a matter of his pride. If he was going to stay, then he wanted to feel like a partner, not a hired hand, not a guy working for room and board who sometimes needed to be guided through things and taught to read. He needed this for his sense of self-worth.

But she resisted, anyway. It didn't seem right to her. He was doing so much to fix up the place, and fixing up this place, as she'd learned, was darn near a full-time job. Catching up was going to take even more time. She needed his help, not his money.

But he was insisting. Partner, not handyman.

"Those are your terms?" she asked.

"Yeah. I don't feel right the way things are. Call me crazy, but it's how I feel."

So he definitely needed to contribute more than sweat and labor. Her heart swelled a bit as she recognized just how overly decent he was. And as she realized he wouldn't settle unless he felt he was on fair footing.

"You're a remarkable man," she said finally.

He shook his head. "Just need to do what's right."

That gave her something to think about. She certainly didn't want him to feel as if he were taking advantage of her, even though he wasn't. On the other hand...

"Have you considered," she asked, "that I might feel I'm taking advantage of you? You already do so much."

"I do damn little when you come right down to it. Some manual labor that I need at least as much as you do. Working hard helps me to feel better. I can't just hang around. What I'm asking for here is a fair deal. If you want me to stay."

If she wanted him to stay. A fair deal. He was talking in business terms right now, and that hurt. She didn't think of this as a business relationship.

"Is that how you see me? As part of a business deal?"

He swore. "Damn it, no! That's the last thing I think of when I think of you. See? I can't even make myself clear. I'm always hurting you somehow. I should just go."

Her chest squeezed until she thought she couldn't draw breath. Her heart began to hammer. There it was again. She sucked air into that constricted place and said angrily, "There's something we need to clear up right now before we go one step further."

"What's that?"

"You've got to stop threatening to leave."

"Threatening? I only mean..."

"I don't care what you mean. It's hitting me like a threat! You want to talk about hurting me? Every time you give me a reason you should leave, that hurts. It hurts badly."

His mouth opened a little. He looked surprised. "I don't mean it that way."

"Maybe not. But that's what it sounds like. Have I asked you to leave? No. But you keep coming up with excuses to go. I can't take that, Liam. I simply can't take that."

"I keep trying to think about what's best for you!"

"Well, that's not good for me in any way. I don't want to wake up some morning to find you've just vanished. Or see you take one of your walks and never come back. God, that would kill me!"

As soon as she said it, she knew it was true. One way or another, she had reached a point where she couldn't imagine life without Liam. "You've got to stop," she said again, as her eyes began to burn with tears. "Just stop saying it and thinking it. Please."

The silence that followed was agonizing.

Then he said, "Okay. I won't talk about it and I won't think about it unless you say you want me to go."

Then she felt awful. "I don't want to force you to stay. That's not what I mean!"

"Hell." He rubbed his chin. He paced one circle in the kitchen, his leg hitching slightly as always. "I get the feeling I keep saying everything wrong. We seem to be cross-talking here. Can I try again?"

She nodded.

"Okay." He faced her. "I don't want to leave. That's not the issue. The issue is whether this is right for you. That's the only issue. Do you really want me hanging around long-term?"

It was as if a stillness came over her heart, and with

it came a certainty. "I don't want you to leave. I'm sure of that, Liam."

"Okay, then. I don't want to leave, either. But you've got to agree to let me help out financially around here or I won't be comfortable. That's all I'm asking."

Insisting more like, she thought, her heart lifting a bit. "I can deal with that," she agreed.

"Okay, then, it's settled. I won't talk about leaving anymore, and I certainly don't want to. Was that clear enough?"

Not quite. She wanted more than a handyman. But he hadn't even suggested it. Even as her heart lifted, her stomach sank. He'd stay, but she knew with absolute conviction that she didn't just want a partner in running the ranch. She wanted ever so much more.

Hardly realizing it, she stepped toward him. She reached out a hand to him, then she caught herself and let it fall. She needed *him* to make the move.

He'd seen the aborted move, though, and a smile began to creep across his face. "You, too, huh?"

She didn't have a chance to ask him what he meant because he closed the distance, wrapped her in his powerful arms and picked her up, then headed for the stairs.

"I'm becoming very fond of you," he muttered as he climbed. "In fact, I want you more than ever."

That was fine by her. Her heart began to sing as it hadn't sung in a long time.

The day's fading light poured through the window to wrap around them as they fell naked onto the bed, but Sharon felt as if they were wrapped in a golden glow. When his staff sank into her body, she felt a sense of completion and wholeness she hadn't felt in forever. This was right, so very right.

And later, when they lay damp and sated, all tangled up on the bed, she burrowed into him as if she could get inside him and never leave.

She wanted this to never end. Never.

"I probably shouldn't say this," he murmured, "but I love you."

Her heart nearly stopped, then skittered as it began to pound. "Why shouldn't you say that?"

"Because it's not fair to you."

She reared up on one elbow, tossing her hair back, and glared at him. Funny to be so angry when every cell in her body was feeling heavy and happy and replete. "Stop worrying about what's fair to me. Let *me* do that, okay?"

His smile was lazy. "Okay. You sure can get mad on a dime. I think I just said something nice to you."

"Then you qualified it. Stop it. And while you're at it, say it again."

"Which part?"

Her anger dissipated as she heard his teasing tone. She playfully swatted his shoulder. "You damn well know which part."

"I love you," he said without qualification. "Maybe you don't…"

She put her hand over his mouth. "Shh. I've been doing nothing but thinking about this, trying to think about what was fair and best for both of us."

"We both seem to have that failing," he remarked from behind her fingers.

"No kidding. Anyway, I'm glad you love me, because, damn it, I love you, too. I want a life with you, Liam. Just the way you are. I can't imagine waking in the morning and not seeing you. I can't imagine a day without you. I wasn't kidding when I said it would kill me if you just left."

He grabbed her then, squeezing her so tightly that she squeaked. At once he loosened his grip. "Sorry, I guess you need to breathe."

The laughter bubbled up in her then and spilled forth. Never had she believed she would be so happy again.

He rolled her over until he was propped on his elbows above her. Smiling, he looked down into her eyes.

"I only want one promise."

She rolled her eyes. "Let me guess. I'll tell you to go if I get fed up."

"I wasn't going to make it that easy. Not now."

A smile lifted her mouth. "Then what?"

"We don't have kids right away. In case. I mean, I want you to be sure I'd be a good father."

She thought about it. "There's time." This time there'd be plenty of time. She was sure of it. "Anything else?"

"We name our first son Chet."

Her breath caught. Then she whispered, "Yes, of course."

"Chet Majors O'Connor. That's okay?"

"That's very okay. Chet would like that."

"I'm not asking Chet. I'm asking you."

"I like it, too."

"And someday we'll tell him the story. But anyway, what do you want from me?"

She looped her arms around his neck and looked into those light green eyes that had both maddened her and given her life's most precious gift: joy. "That you'll never leave me. That you'll be here every single day."

"I promise."

"Then I'll take that as a marriage proposal."

He laughed, looking happier than she'd ever seen him. "And your answer is?"

"Yes, Liam. Very definitely yes."

They came together again, this time slowly, lingering over each new touch. The passion built gradually, growing steadily until it became a white-hot blaze.

They'd come home, Sharon thought. At last, they had both found a home. With each other.

Then she gave herself up to the future.

* * * * *

REQUEST YOUR FREE BOOKS!

2 FREE NOVELS PLUS 2 FREE GIFTS!

⊕ HARLEQUIN®

SPECIAL EDITION

Life, Love & Family

YES! Please send me 2 FREE Harlequin® Special Edition novels and my 2 FREE gifts (gifts are worth about $10). After receiving them, if I don't wish to receive any more books, I can return the shipping statement marked "cancel." If I don't cancel, I will receive 6 brand-new novels every month and be billed just $4.74 per book in the U.S. or $5.24 per book in Canada. That's a savings of at least 14% off the cover price! It's quite a bargain! Shipping and handling is just 50¢ per book in the U.S. and 75¢ per book in Canada.* I understand that accepting the 2 free books and gifts places me under no obligation to buy anything. I can always return a shipment and cancel at any time. Even if I never buy another book, the two free books and gifts are mine to keep forever.

235/335 HDN F45Y

Name	(PLEASE PRINT)	
Address		Apt. #
City	State/Prov.	Zip/Postal Code

Signature (if under 18, a parent or guardian must sign)

Mail to the **Harlequin® Reader Service:**
IN U.S.A.: P.O. Box 1867, Buffalo, NY 14240-1867
IN CANADA: P.O. Box 609, Fort Erie, Ontario L2A 5X3

Want to try two free books from another line?
Call 1-800-873-8635 or visit www.ReaderService.com.

* Terms and prices subject to change without notice. Prices do not include applicable taxes. Sales tax applicable in N.Y. Canadian residents will be charged applicable taxes. Offer not valid in Quebec. This offer is limited to one order per household. Not valid for current subscribers to Harlequin Special Edition books. All orders subject to credit approval. Credit or debit balances in a customer's account(s) may be offset by any other outstanding balance owed by or to the customer. Please allow 4 to 6 weeks for delivery. Offer available while quantities last.

Your Privacy—The Harlequin® Reader Service is committed to protecting your privacy. Our Privacy Policy is available online at www.ReaderService.com or upon request from the Harlequin Reader Service.

We make a portion of our mailing list available to reputable third parties that offer products we believe may interest you. If you prefer that we not exchange your name with third parties, or if you wish to clarify or modify your communication preferences, please visit us at www.ReaderService.com/consumerschoice or write to us at Harlequin Reader Service Preference Service, P.O. Box 9062, Buffalo, NY 14269. Include your complete name and address.

HSE13R

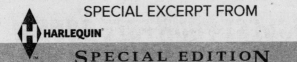
Handsome carpenter Dean Pritchett comes to Rust Creek Falls to help rebuild the town after the Great Montana Flood and meets a younger woman with a checkered past. Can Shelby Jenkins repair the damage to this cowboy's heart?

***

Shelby laid a hand on his arm. "Please, don't stop. I like listening to you."

"Yeah?"

She nodded, trying to erase the tingling sensation that danced from her palm to her elbow thanks to the warmth of his skin.

"My brothers and I have worked on projects together, but usually it's just me and whatever piece of furniture I'm working on."

"Solitary sounds good to me. My job is nothing but working with people. Sometimes that can be hard, too."

"Especially when those people aren't so nice?"

Shelby nodded, wrapping her arms around her bent knees as she stared out at the nearby creek.

Dean leaned closer, brushing back the hair that had fallen against her cheek, his thumb staying behind to move back and forth across her cheek.

Her breath caught, then vanished completely the moment he touched her. She was frozen in place, her arms locked around her knees, held captive by the simple press of his thumb.

He gently lifted her head while lowering his. The warmth of